Inspired by a True Story

ISAAC

By ROBERT KARMON

PLEASURE BOAT STUDIO

ISBN 978-0-912887-53-1

Library of Congress Control Number: 2017940930

Cover and Interior Design by Lauren Grosskopf

Pleasure Boat Studio books are available through your favorite bookstore
and through the following:
SPD (Small Press Distribution) Tel. 800-869-7553
Baker & Taylor 800-775-1100
Ingram Tel 615-793-5000
Amazon.com and bn.com

and through
PLEASURE BOAT STUDIO: A LITERARY PRESS
www.pleasureboatstudio.com
Seattle, Washington

Contact Lauren Grosskopf, Publisher
Email: Lrslate88@gmail.com

"The masterfulness of Robert Karmon's story-telling is revealed in his ability to render Isaac's survival in all its rawness and creativeness. We should all greet that, like Isaac, with a basket of oranges."

~MARIO SUSKO, author of *"The Auxilliary time of being"*

"This riveting novel tells the story of Isaac, a sixteen-year-old boy who miraculously survived the 1941 massacre of over 20,000 Jews in Rovno, Poland. Karmon tells the tale of Isaac's harrowing escape in prose that is evocative, beautiful and precise. Through it all, Isaac survives by his resourcefulness and courage, while experiencing the exhiliration (and painful loss) of his first love. It is a coming of age story, unlike any other, but it is not only that. It is a tribute to the human spirit. Karmon's book belongs on every shelf of the best of Holocaust literature."

~ROBERT SECOR, English Professor Emeritus, Vice-Provost of Penn State.

ISAAC

Dedication

Without the constant love and support of my dear
wife, Kay, this book, *Isaac,* would not have survived.
Deeply thankful as well for the supportive presence of
my entire family: my children, Elysa and Jennifer; their
wonderful husbands, Harry and John, and the charms
and smiles of my grandchildren, Jesse, Zoe and Elle.
Special thanks to my constant friend and advocate
for this book, Louis Phillips.

The past is never dead, it's not even past.

— WILLIAM FAULKNER, from *"Requiem for a Nun."*

To the indomitable spirit of Isaac

CHAPTER ONE
SIX KILOS

When Isaac came home from school and saw that the millstones had stopped turning, he knew the war had finally come to Rovno. Three months before, on July 21st, Germany had invaded Russian territory and plunged Eastern Poland into combat. But until this final week of September 1941, Rovno had been spared the scars of battle.

In the house, his father acted nonchalant, convinced that the situation was only temporary. Tanning and curing would resume once the workers returned, but for now, with the Germans pushing towards the town, everyone had fled.

For the next few days, the family went about their business tensely; Hindle and Aunt Rifka baking breads, pumping water in reserve, cleaning and airing the blankets and linens; while at night, Lazar and Isaac would sit looking at old album pictures. A picture of Lazar in his old Russian uniform provoked a mixture of pride and laughter in Lazar, but Isaac, only sixteen, saw in the youthful romantic features of his young father the sketchy outline of his own face. While father and son rummaged through yellowing photos, the women slept, to awaken before sunrise and begin cleaning and cooking all over again.

After a week, Lazar broke the tension of the family, as they waited each day for the war to arrive. He stood up at the dinner table and declared, "We have nothing to worry about. What can happen? If they take away our tanning plant, we still have our lands, we will have our house; if they seize our house, I've hidden enough money away by the well and in the stone fence to keep us secure in some other country; and if they find the money and take our possessions, we are still a family and we can start over."

Aunt Rifka, nervous and unsure, broke out suddenly in tears and ran from the room. Hindle kissed her husband proudly and Isaac marveled at his father's spirit and courage.

The next morning, the roar of planes could be heard. Later, the whine and grind of tanks echoed in the distance to the south. Then Isaac heard the snort of gunfire for the first time, machine guns crackling like wet wood in a roaring hearth, and soon spumes of flame and ashy funnels of smoke could be seen rising above the western horizon.

By night, the western sky glowed like red embers, and the sound of planes overhead increased, with the thud and rumble of falling bombs felt underneath the ground.

For the next few days, while Russian troops and German divisions fought on the outskirts of town, Isaac could see crowds of townspeople escaping in the distance, along the Narew Road toward Kiev. It was reported that the fighting grew so fierce, it spilled out into the streets of Rovno itself, with both sides advancing and retreating from hour to hour. Rovno was on the road to Moscow and Warsaw, and both armies wanted control.

From the window of the house, the war still seemed a fiery canvas in the distance, but the constant rumble of falling artillery shells and bombs grew stronger, the whine of tanks louder.

Then suddenly it all stopped. It was the beginning of October and the fighting had gone on for a week, but suddenly there was silence, except for a distant crackle of gunfire.

No workers returned, the millstone remained still, but Lazar was convinced it was over, so he started to tour his plant once again, checking machinery, looking for damage.

By the second day of this new tranquility, the radio returned to the air, with a German announcer declaring victory of the elite Nazi divisions and proclaiming the Polish people safe from Bolshevik oppression forever.

The following day, Sol felt it was safe enough to return to his clinic and resume his work. Isaac was allowed to accompany his brother and help in any way he could.

Approaching Skolynia Road leading to the clinic and the heart of Rovno, Isaac could see the remnants of battle: charred foundations, collapsed roofs, gaping bomb craters and smoking rubble but the town still remained, for the most part, recognizable and untouched.

Even Sol's clinic had been spared, and already the patients were waiting, casualities of war. They huddled and crouched by the entrance and up the stairs leading to the front door, wretched figures in blood-spattered rags or shivering beneath muddy blankets. Sol quickly opened the door and, with Lyuba's and Isaac's help, the clinic was soon warm and bright, the staff ministering to the wounded.

During a lull, Lyuba sent Isaac upstairs into the library to rest and eat some stew she had warmed up from the night before. Once again, entering the second floor library, Isaac felt renewed confidence and security. From the window, he looked out over unusually empty streets and just beyond, towards the surrounding hills where puffs of ashy smoke still rose in the air.

Settling back, Isaac began looking for a new book, a new text. As he was looking, he heard a commotion downstairs in the hallway. He went to the door, opened it slightly and peered down the stairs through the crack. From his vantage point, he could see a German officer in a black uniform with leather straps and a tan cap. The officer was gesturing angrily at Lyuba, ordering in German that the patients be removed from the clinic. Since Isaac understood German perfectly, along with five other languages, he had no difficulty following the exchange.

Lyuba looked shocked, frightened, but was reluctant to follow the officer's command. Then the officer, with a name like Bingel or Bichel, slapped his leather gloves sharply in his palm and shouted out an order to his soldiers waiting outside. More soldiers appeared and began to herd the patients out of the hallway, shoving them rudely off the benches with the butt of their guns. At that point, Lyuba ran to get Sol. He emerged, outraged and indignant.

"You have no authority to do such a thing!" Sol's voice was high pitched, intense.

The officer looked at the thin, handsome face of the doctor, still dressed in his white jacket. "I am the only authority, pig!"

But Sol was not listening. Instead, he tried to stop the soldier from shoving a woman out the door. She looked befuddled and unsteady, her one arm wrapped in a blood-soaked linen, her face sallow from the loss of blood.

"Get your hands off her. She is in shock, don't you see?"

But as Sol tried to grab the soldier and pull him away, the officer stepped in and slapped Sol across the face, so hard it drove him back against the bench. Isaac had never seen his brother treated with anything but reverence and respect. The physical assault on him seemed unreal, like an episode from some fictional tale.

Sol rubbed his face, straightened up, and held his temper. "I insist that I be allowed to carry out my medical duties."

The German officer, a Commandant in Einsatzgruppen C, laughed. "He insists. Do you hear that?" The soldiers laughed in turn, savage, raucous laughter.

The Commandant continued. "Now I will tell you what you must do. Some of my troops need immediate transfusions. We will round up the youngest children and you will draw blood from them to supply my wounded."

Sol looked at him grimly. "Children? You want me to take

blood from the children?"

"From infants, if possible! I don't want to weaken the able-bodied men in town. We will need them immediately, so infants and children will do."

"I cannot take blood from babies. It would kill them. Let me find you healthy young volunteers. I will gladly treat your men."

"You will not touch my soldiers. A German doctor will care for the German wounded. Your job will be with the babies here, collecting blood."

Sol shook his head, desperate and exasperated. "I cannot. I won't kill some child."

"You cannot?" The Commandant shouted at him. Lyuba moved closer to her husband, taking his arm firmly, protectively. She was frightened. Isaac could see that in her eyes.

"One last time, pig. I order you to take blood from the youngest volunteers we can find, infants if possible."

Sol looked down, paused, took Lyuba's hand and clutched it for support. "I want to help you and your men in whatever way I can, sir. But I am sure that your own doctors would not agree to such an order."

The Commandant stiffened. "You will not obey?"

"In all conscience," Sol started to explain almost tenderly and patiently, "I am first a doctor and could not . . ."

Before he had finished his sentence, it happened. So quickly, Isaac did not have time to turn away, but watched intently. As Sol quietly explained his objections, the Commandant unsnapped his side holster, drew his revolver, aimed it directly at Sol's face and pulled the trigger. His motion was so fluid, so smooth and unhesitating, it looked as if he were only shaking Sol's hand or brushing a cinder off Sol's face. But the shot was real and Isaac could feel the echo of the bullet vibrate in the door he held ajar. Sol's head jerked backwards like it was all cloth and sawdust, and his whole body instantly collapsed into a heap.

At first Isaac did not associate the gunshot with his brother, nor did he connect the spray of blood on Lyuba's skirt or on the Commandant's uniform with Sol. Then Lyuba began to scream and she kneeled down at Sol's limb body, shaking him, pounding his shoulders.

While she cried out and struggled to shake life back into her husband's body, the Commandant signaled to one of the soldiers to remove both Sol and Lyuba. When the soldier grabbed Lyuba, she turned on him, punching and kicking. Another soldier came up and without a pause, slammed the butt of his rifle across the side of her head. The sound of the impact made Isaac turn. His stomach quivered in disgust, his whole body winced and revolted, but he dared not scream out. It was over, and both Lyuba and Sol were dragged away by their feet like empty sacks.

With a look of disgust, the Commandant shouted, "Burn this place. It's useless."

Still undetected, Isaac kneeled, holding back the scream of grief and horror. His body was shaking uncontrollably and his fingers were numb from gripping the door so fiercely. Part of him wanted to rush down and rescue his loved ones, but another part—the frightened and vigilant voice inside him— kept reminding him to run, to escape. With the sound of soldiers returning carrying pitch-tar torches, smashing windows, kicking down doors, Isaac erupted into action and ran to the back of the library where a small attic window promised escape. With his heart racing, he scrambled through the window and slid down the sloping back roof, kicking up shingles as he slid down. But no one heard him over the noise of the soldiers setting fire to the clinic.

On the ground Isaac began to run, not looking back or to

the side, but instinctively toward home just as the sound of flames roared through the clinic. Isaac kept running, crying and screaming inside, but never once stopping to rest.

When he finally saw his house, he collapsed to his knees, breathless, and crawled the last few meters to the front door.

Hindle saw her son first, his clothes torn and soiled, his face streaked and sobbing, but when he finally quieted down and tried to explain what he had seen, he broke out in tears again, choking on his words, unable and unwilling to remember.

Even when he managed to piece the story together, it still didn't seem real. Hindle protested. "You are talking about German officers. Lazar, you spent a whole year with such soldiers. They are not monsters. This is not possible . . . not possible."

She held Isaac close while Lazar wiped off his face with a wet cloth. Aunt Rifka had retreated into the darkness of the sitting room, frightened by Isaac's story. She started to pray to her late husband, crying to him in the dark. All that night following Sol's murder, Isaac and his family sat up in the main room, nodding off to sleep, then awakening suddenly with a start, afraid of what morning might bring. The stillness through the long night was broken only by uncontrollable sobbing, first by Isaac as his body shook off the nightmare, then Hindle, realizing her Sol was gone forever. And in the other room, Isaac's aunt could be heard, muttering to herself and praying to the shadowy corners.

With morning, Lazar went to the door and looked out. Across the road, he could see a long column of young men —some had been workers at his plant—carrying shovels and picks, led by Ukrainian police and SS officers. But Lazar hesitated to confront any of them, unsure of the soldiers or the police. Later that day, an older worker came to the door. He had been employed by Lazar for many years and felt a certain loyalty to the family. He seemed anxious to come inside before anyone saw him paying a visit to Lazar's home, but once inside the house, and with a glass of cider, he relaxed. From him, Lazar learned that the young men he'd seen this morning were on their way to the Sosenki region to dig anti-tank trenches against a possible counter-attack by the Bolsheviks. The trenches would take a week to complete and meanwhile, the Einsatzgruppen C commando force, sent by Himmler into this region, would attempt to relocate the almost 20,000 Jews to protect them from retaliation by local anti-Semitic groups. Without the protection of the Russian army, the Jews were in a vulnerable position, and the German high command planned to resettle the Jewish inhabitants in some location more easily defended against such attacks.

Lazar listened with a certain amount of relief. At least the fighting was over and his family would remain together. When the worker left, he shook everyone's hand, kissed Hindle goodbye, and quickly departed.

For three days Isaac's family remained sequestered by choice in their house. Lazar had drawn all the curtains and he lit only the most necessary candles. Even with the Sukkoth festival approaching, Lazar felt reluctant to contact his other Jewish friends, and decided instead to wait out the events. No one else visited them until a week passed. Then there was a heavy knock on the kitchen door. When Hindle looked through the window, she saw her neighbor, the Polish fireman. She opened it gratefully and let him in.

"Are you leaving yet?"

Hindle looked at him. "We are not planning a trip."

"I heard from my cousin in town. He is in the new police battalion organized by the SS. All Jews will be traveling East for resettlement." The fireman spoke with a tone of self-satisfied pleasure. He seemed to be relishing all the gossip that was spreading.

"We haven't been informed."

Lazar stood by the kitchen entrance. He felt no desire to invite the fireman in. There was something about this visit that offended him.

"Eventually, my friends, eventually, the Nazis will take everything. The house, the furnishings, and give it away or store it or sell it. Look, my wife and I love that gilded mirror in the hallway and that painting of some kind of wildflowers in the study. We thought you'd rather give it to friends that have it go to strangers."

Hindle listened with increasing rage while Lazar calmly approached the fireman and crowded him toward the door. "We are not yet ready to leave. And we have no intentions of selling any of our possessions."

"Sell? You have no chance to sell any of this. You're lucky if you can give it away before the Nazis take it. I just thought you'd rather..."

Lazar opened the door, practically pushing the fireman out, gritting his teeth in anger as he spoke. "I thank you for your thoughtfulness. If we ever decide to give away some of our belongings, I'm sure we'll give you and your lovely wife first consideration."

The fireman grinned, reared back haughtily and snarled, "You're fools. I give you a choice. Tomorrow you won't have a choice. You're not big shots anymore. You're nothing. Nothing!"

And the door slammed forever on the face of their neighbor. Hindle sat down, shaking, apprehensive. Lazar laughed it off and went back into the darkened study to sit and take stock of his house and all it contained. These last few days had found him taking inventory, over and over, almost as if to reassure himself that it was still his house.

The next morning, everyone heard the sound of trucks and

lorries and voices in the distance. Isaac looked out first and saw thousands of people walking on the Narew Road, carrying small suitcases or a child or both. They wore thick coats and were guarded on each side by Ukrainian police and German soldiers. All through the morning, people walked the distant road. It seemed to never end and Isaac would peer out from behind the curtains from hour to hour expecting to see the people gone. Instead, they grew in numbers.

But by late afternoon, it was obvious all of Rovno's Jews were on the road, and columns of Jews would go by relentlessly through the day. Their voices were muted, just faint, distant murmurs, while an occasional military vehicle would crash by or some line of heavily ladened trucks or lorries could be heard speeding alongside the endless procession.

Near evening, there was a knock on the door. Lazar stood, his body tense. The knock grew heavier. When he opened it, a German officer in a starched and spotless uniform entered, saluted with his arm upraised, his fist gripping leather gloves, and then quietly took Lazar aside. The family stood back in the corner of the main room, afraid to be seen. In a matter of minutes, the officer walked bristly out, saluting with an upraised arm once again, leaving Lazar to organize his family.

It was quite simple and precise. Just as the worker had warned, the Jewish population was to be resettled immediately in order to insure their safety. Each Jewish member of the household would be allowed to leave with no more than six kilos. Everything else must be left behind; but, Lazar had been promised, property and possessions would be protected until safe return.

"You were right, Hindle. They are not monsters. It sounds quite orderly and civilized to me."

Hindle did not respond, but quickly went about her business. Lazar had been informed that the squad leader for their region would be coming by later that night to accompany them to their relocation point, and proper transportation would be provided. They had to be ready to travel in a few hours, standing outside with their six kilos.

Silently, almost with a certain resignation and resolve, Isaac's family quickly packed. Hindle first helped her son, putting into a small cloth suitcase only the necessary clothing, some hard bread wrapped in newspaper, and soap. When Isaac attempted to place his Zayda's cane into the suitcase, Hindle stopped him.

"We'll come back later for the cane. It will be safe. I promise."

Isaac was shocked. To leave behind such a precious legacy seemed almost sacrilegious to him, but he felt so helpless and confused at this point, whatever his parents said to do, he would follow. It did not seem like some kind of new adventure. It felt wrong. A sickening kind of heat rose up in his belly, and a tense heaviness settled in his chest, forcing him to breathe more deliberately. His whole body was tightening as he waited in his room, holding his grandfather's cane, playing with the worn brass handle that had been rubbed by his Zayda's strong firm hands in decades past. He sat on his bed, clutching the cane to his chest, resting his head on the handle, and stared into the darkness of rooms beyond his doorway.

Then he heard a truck and a Kübelwagen, a jeep-like military vehicle, and voices outside. There were shouts, orders, and suddenly Hindle appeared. She rushed into the room, putting her finger to her lip, and with the other hand pressed two objects into his palm. Then she kissed him, and, just as silently, walked out, indicating that it was time to leave. He looked into his hand and saw two gold rings. Somehow he understood that he was to keep them safe, and he quickly placed them on his fingers, so that they would not fall off. Then he picked up his cloth suitcase and walked out of his room, glancing back at the cane, as if he were abandoning some living friend. It leaned against his bedstead as it had for months.

His family was waiting for him at the door, each one carrying a meager suitcase filled up to the precious six kilos allowed. Together they walked out into the swarming activity of the night.

They were met by glaring headlamps, shouts, a truck growling past covered with a powdery whiteness that smelled acrid and strong. Then a military vehicle pulled up and a tall, slim German officer jumped out and ordered Lazar to find a place in the line. He pointed to the left and when they looked, Isaac's family could make out an endless crowd of townspeople, shoulder to shoulder, huddling, shivering in the cold night air, all carrying their six kilos of treasures. Isaac had never seen so many people gathered together at once. The faces stretched out toward the distant road, more numberless than the trees. Everyone moved slowly but methodically, with soldiers flanking them on all sides, rifles strapped to their shoulders, shouting out commands to move faster when the place slackened.

Lazar grabbed his son's arm and drew him close, and then took his wife's hand and held it tightly. He waited until Aunt Rifka was alongside as well, and then they started out in the chilly, moonlit night.

The Germans had divided the Jewish inhabitants into groups of five hundred, by region, geography, and economic rank. Isaac's family, according to this system, had been selected to join the last group. Behind them Isaac could see a convoy of trucks, all piled high with material in the back, covered with canvas and kicking up clouds of white powder in their wake. At first, Lazar set the pace, walking slowly and deliberately, as if he were on a hike in the countryside with his son once again. But the chill of the night and the fearful white of the faces all about him, along with the deadly, sullen quiet of the marchers, made it clear to Isaac this was no ordinary hike.

An hour into the walk and Aunt Rifka started to breathe painfully. She grabbed Lazar's arm and knelt to catch her breath. But when Lazar stopped to help, a soldier stepped up to them and pushed them on with his rifle.

"My aunt is exhausted. Let her rest."

Lazar pleaded but the German soldier shook his head and tapped Aunt Rifka on the shoulder with the rifle butt. She looked up, saw the cold indifference of the young soldier's face, and quickly stood up. She did not pause again, remembering the touch of the rifle against her shoulder.

In this night-long journey, military vehicles would pass up and down, stopping, with soldiers running to receive messages from the driver, then starting up to speed them toward town. Behind Isaac, the trucks kept a steady pace, always on the heels of the marchers.

Once or twice, Isaac heard someone cry out for assistance, and then he thought he saw a figure running toward the bushes for relief. The crowd passed the spot where the figure had vanished and then, a few minutes later, Isaac heard what sounded like the crack of a whip or the snapping of branches in an ice storm. He couldn't make it out, but he saw his father shudder and he felt his father's grip tighten on his own hand. Each time some poor person cried out for some assistance and was allowed to leave the ranks and vanish in the brush at the side of the road, the group would pass the figure and never see that person again.

The soldiers kept urging the people on, forcing them to maintain the pace. After two hours of walking slowly and dragging the weight of six kilos along, Isaac could hear new sounds in the distance. He thought at first it was some screeching owl or a baying wolf. They were approaching the Sosenki and the noise of that great forest always filled with animal sounds at night. But these cries in the distance and the sounds, the electric crackle followed by a booming echo, were unmistakable. These were human voices crying out, and the other sounds were gunshots.

With that realization and the sight of the white birches appearing dimly under the moonlight, Isaac listened as the soldiers shouted new orders. They were orders blurted out in three languages—German, Polish, Ukrainian. Isaac understood all of them. The message was the same.

"Stop. Put down your luggage. Place it at the side of the road and undress. Immediately. Now!"

Lazar looked startled. Others turned to him questioningly and he tried to approach an officer to inquire what this new command meant. But as he left the road, the soldier lifted his rifle to his shoulder, pointing it at Lazar. "Get back in line and undress." He was a young Ukrainian from a nearby village, and his rifle shook nervously in his hand. Lazar retreated back.

Again the sound of animal-like screeches and cries, followed by that icy snap of electricity, a sudden crackle, and the jolt of an echo reverberating over the heads of everyone.

They did not move now, but the soldiers came at them with guns and pistols, pushing, slapping, forcing them to undress and ripping the luggage from their hands. Isaac's aunt could not stand it any longer and fell to her knees, crying. Hindle helped her up just before the soldiers spotted her and then, almost with a motherly tenderness, Hindle began to unbutton her blouse. Aunt Rifka did not protest. Everyone about her had begun to undress under the lashing voices and gestures of the soldiers. But Isaac could not look. A wave of nausea and embarrassment swept over him. He was both terrified and humiliated, and for a moment, his fingers seemed paralyzed, unable to open shirts or unbuckle pants. Lazar saw this and came toward him. He embraced his son and Isaac, pressing close to his father's chest, could hear the pounding of his heart. He had never heard his father's heart before and it was like some animal in flight, racing out of control. When he looked up, Lazar was crying, but he smiled at his son and kissed him. Then he turned to his wife, took her in his arms and kissed her many times. They were half undressed by now, stumbling, groping in the dark, and all about, Isaac could hear cries and sobs, the heaving of the sick, the shrieks and plaintive appeals to loved ones and to God.

The movement became even more regimented. Solders appeared at their back, kicking away the luggage and pushing their naked bodies forward toward a dark shadowy area just beyond the rise. In all the confusion Isaac did not see nakedness, just the fear in the eyes, the horror and degradation in the mouth. He was cold, and his mother, her skin beautiful and smooth in the smoky moonlight, put her arm around Isaac. Whatever shame Isaac might have felt vanished. He just wanted to be as near to his mother and father as he could be in these harrowing and bewildering moments.

Then the screams began again and just ahead Isaac could see, stretched out in a row, left and right of him as far as he could make out in the moonlight, double lines of naked bodies, cowering, clutching themselves in the last desperate gestures of modesty. Behind him, SS officers and Ukrainian police stood with revolvers drawn, rifles pointed and machine guns readied. The trucks and the military vehicles shined their headlamps on the bodies, and with a shout up and down the line, the firing began. The bodies jolted forward with the crack of the bullets and vanished into the earth. Isaac could not see that far ahead, but in the glare of the headlights, he could make out the details of the horror. His body was flushed with a sudden heat, a fever that made him sweat suddenly, then shake. His throat tightened, until he could not speak or swallow.

Crowding closer to his father and mother, he looked around

for some sign of reality. This was happening so fast, so systematically, it was like he had been caught up in someone else's life.

Another double line formed and the soldiers pushed Isaac and his parents farther toward the front and the blazing lights. There were screams and shrieking all about now, before the round of gunshots and after. It was maddening, deafening. Not far from Isaac, a child of three was ripped from his mother's arms and the mother was shoved forward toward the front. She screamed and reached for the child, but the soldier tossed the child into the air and it fell, disappearing into the darkness up ahead.

Another volley of shots—machine guns, revolvers, rifles—and with a hideous regularity, the next two lines of naked bodies were thrust forward.

Isaac could now see all the way in front. Just beyond the victims stood a gaping trench, the one that took the workers a week to dig. It was filled with bodies in the most horrible postures of death. Arms jutted out, eyes stared in shock, torso pressed down on torso with such enormity that infants and the smallest children were simply tossed in letting the fatal weight of the adult bodies on top crush and suffocate them.

When Isaac looked up, he saw his father's face in the light, strangely defiant, jaw set hard. Even in his nakedness, Lazar displayed no shame. It was their turn next. The gunmen were in a hurry. Some had grown weary, some almost crazed by the constant slaughter. Many had already opened cardboard suitcases and cloth satchels to search for valuables and money, scattering clothes and personal belongings into the air. But the killing continued with demonic efficiency.

It was at that moment, Lazar broke the line, grabbed a young German soldier standing at the trench, and demanded "Kill me first! Now! I don't want to see my family killed. Do it now!"

He grabbed the leather belt strapped diagonal across the

soldier's chest, practically pulling him into the bloody trench. But the soldier regained his balance and shoved Lazar back, angrily. He stumbled into the arms of Hindle, who held him tearfully. Isaac could not bear the look of such pain and suffering in the faces of his father and mother. He could not stand the sight of horror one more second, and he rushed forward, breaking from the line, hurling himself at the same soldier his father had just confronted. The German gunman was caught off guard, a look of panic in his eyes. Practically clutching at the soldier's collar, Isaac shouted insistently, almost angrily, "I can't stand seeing my parents die. Kill me ... now!"

For a brief second, he caught sight of the vulnerable figures of his parents with this aunt behind them, her back to the trenches, unable to contemplate the nightmare. In that instant, as Isaac tried to fix the image of his loved ones in his mind forever, the young German gunman pushed him away in a rage, raised his revolver, aimed hurriedly at Isaac's head and squeezed the trigger. There was a thunderous roar. The revolver spent its shell, and then all sound stopped abruptly as Isaac dropped into unconsciousness.

CHAPTER TWO
DOGSKIN AND GOLD

In the darkness of the trench, Isaac moved his hands over the strange texture of the dead. He did not know what he touched first. How could he? By the end of that chilly October night, on the second day of Sukkoth—the festival of harvest and thanksgiving—the Nazi Einsatzkommando units, with the help of Ukrainian police, had murdered over 20,000 Jewish citizens of Rovno. What could Isaac ever know of that, lying unconscious in what should have been his grave through one full day and into the evening?

He couldn't know of Rabbi Mahofit and his refusal to live even when a Nazi captain offered to spare his life. All that was asked of the rabbi was to return to his Rovno synagogue and console the remaining Jews in their new ghetto and to lie about what he'd seen. Just lie and console. But Rabbi Mahofit strode to the edge of the burial trench and declared that his place was there, down there in the grave with his people. That was his answer. He was stripped quickly of his sacred vestments and shot.

As for his friend Morris, Isaac could never know of or even imagine his death. It was Morris who tried to save his people. Always nervous and suspicious, always on the verge of stuttering, Morris could not walk dutifully in line with the others. He had to find out what was ahead. So, bending his tall body from the waist like some fictional thief, he snuck up toward the front, stooping and crouching, head bobbing up and down just out sight of the German soldiers and Ukrainian police patrolling at the sides. Concealed by flanks of marching townspeople, Morris managed to reach a point a half-mile up the line where the terrain rose slightly to a small ridge. Approaching it, Morris thought for certain he would be able to see the embarkation point where the numerous convoys of trucks and personnel vehicles would be assembled to convey his family and friends to a new resettlement camp. Oddly, though, as he climbed the sloping ridge toward the top, he heard disturbing sounds: wailing, shrieks of pain and grief, and a steady, unsettling groan, all punctuated by sharp reports from automatic rifles and pistols. Cracking, explosive sounds would echo off the distant birch trees of the Sosenki and die away, but the cries of grief and pain persisted unwaveringly.

At the top of the rise, Morris hid behind an old man in the line pushing a small wagon piled high with clothing and satchels and food. From behind the wagon, he could see down into the flat plain leading to the white birches in the distance. An unusual mist clung to the ground in the distance, a mist of quicklime, ash and gunfire mixed with the evening dampness. He saw horses yoked to ammunition carts twitching and rearing nervously at each sound, their nostrils snorting and puffing. And then he made out the real activity, the true military "operation." He recognized the naked bodies crowding together and understood the sight of the trench slashing across the landscape like an angry welt scarring Morris' tender memories of the Volhynia plains.

For a minute or two, which was all he could stand, he watched the methodical slaughter, the piling up of personal belongings in heaps behind the soldiers. Then he recoiled. He ran back down the slope, through the middle of the column of people, screaming and waving his arms. His voice cracked; his syllables stumbled and skipped. "T . . . t . . . turn b . . . ba . . . Turn back!" His stuttering increased with his desperation. The townspeople were startled, wary and suspicious of this hysterical young boy tripping over his words, and they tried to avoid him, giving him a wide berth within the line. As Morris rushed through the slowly moving file of Jewish inhabitants toward his family a half-mile away, he continued to shout and wave, "They're mu...mu...murdering everyone! Murdering everyone! I saw it! Be...be...believe me. I saw it!"

A Ukrainian policeman, not much older than Morris, was ordered by a German officer to seize this disruptive boy. Breaking through the line, the policeman quickly subdued the boy, and with the help of other officers, dragged him away towards a waiting personnel truck, its canvas roof slapping loudly with each bump in the road. While they threw Morris into the back of the vehicle, other soldiers went up and down the line of people joking about the boy and his stuttering, hinting that his speech impediment suggested less than competent mental faculties. "P...p...puh! Poor buh...buh...buh...boy!" they mocked. "Puh...puh...poor imbuh...buh...becile! Poor imbecile!" No one laughed back at the officers, but the ridicule distracted the people from the memory of Morris's brief warnings. So the Jewish citizens of Rovno marched on, relentlessly, unable to hear the muffled echo of a pistol shot from inside the canvas-backed personnel truck.

Isaac could never truly know any of this; least of all, imagine in his innocence, how his family died. How his aunt was dragged toward the trench, her body still clenched in a fetal position, her back to the soldiers, refusing to face her murderers or her grave, no matter how hard they kicked her. Eyes closed, knees gripped, muttering in a kind of chant her late husband's name, she was shot through the back of the head and dragged backward into the trench.

Right after Isaac's aunt, his mother was shot abruptly as she reached to grasp Lazar's hand. Lazar, seeing his wife crumple suddenly before him, cried out and rushed forward to cover her fallen body with his own. He thrust himself across her still trembling form, embracing her naked body, trying to keep her warm and comforted. No matter how hard they tried, the soldiers could not wrench Lazar's fingers free from his grip on Hindle's body or force his body off. Finally, they shot him in that position and shoved both bodies into the trench, where Lazar and Hindle fell together, arms and legs entangled.

By the time Hindle and Lazar were killed, the soldiers were nearing the end of their numbing, brutal routine of extermination. They were so exhausted and impatient after all the bloodletting that they grew careless and indifferent in their burial operation. Instead of covering the trenches with a thick layer of chloride of lime, followed by truckloads of dirt and rubble as they did in other sectors, these officers and soldiers cut corners. They were anxious to distribute the clothing in the satchels and suitcases, the litter of personal treasures left by the victims, so they did not worry about proper burial procedure. They just went through the motions perfunctorily, shoving barely enough dirt into the graves to conceal the gorge of blood and bodies beneath.

Further north, in those sectors nearer the Volhynia woods, the Einsatzgruppen leaders made sure that trenches were properly filled with quicklime and dirt. In those areas, local residents would tell of the ground above the trenches rising up and down for many days after the soldiers left, swelling and collapsing as if the earth itself was heaving and gasping for air.

But beneath the thin blanket of soil and the suffocating weight of the bodies in his sector, Isaac somehow remained alive.

The hurried pistol shot aimed at his head had only grazed the orbital bone above his left eye, leaving a shallow gouge across his eyebrow. But the concussion from the bullet's impact left him unconscious for a whole day. It was only by early evening that he began awakening.

First, he moved his hands, then he opened his right eye. He could see dim shadows and a weak yellow light filtering down from above. Then, in the puzzling shadows, he recognized a cheekbone, a nose, an eye staring blankly up in terror.

Dreadful realizations had returned to his memory. His left eye, crusted, closed and throbbing with pain, reminded him of the last pistol shot. Images of the last moments ebbed back. His fingers numbly traced the outline of bodies above and below him. When he tried to push against the bodies and free himself, their rubbery give filled him with nausea. But he kept pushing and groping upwards toward the source of the pale yellow light.

As he slid upward, raising himself from the grave, past the bodies, his right hand touched a gentle slop of cheek, a sharply etched nose and he knew who it was. He knew, but would not look. Unmistakably, he had touched his mother's face. He wanted to burst out crying, but something inside forbade him to make a sound. An exhausted sense of grief, perhaps, or the fatigue of too much pain held back his tears. Or maybe it was a persistent sense of vigilance, an animal-like wariness that kept him silent in the midst of despair. Besides, he could not even cry; his wounded left eye was dry and frozen shut. In fact, Isaac welcomed the pulsating pain in the eye for it quickened his senses and kept his mind focused on each task.

Shrugging off the weight of more bodies, with dirt spilling over his hands and face like rain, he reached the top edge of the trench. There, clinging to the bank of earth, he rested for a moment. He dared not look back or to the side for fear of seeing all the dead and recognizing the faces. Instead, he pressed his face against the soil where twisted roots had been exposed and stayed silent, his heart beating against the clay and undersoil of the trench.

He was sure there would be more soldiers waiting just above him, and he expected a blow to his head or a sharp crack of a pistol at any moment. But he only heard the pounding of his heart and his own quick and shallow breathing.

Gathering strength once again, he pulled his naked body out of the trench, flinging forward, flattening his body on the ground, always expecting the bark of a German officer and the sharp report of some weapon aimed at his head. Again, there was nothing: no movement, no sounds. He raised his body to one knee and looked ahead. The Nazis and their gunmen had left. In the darkness, Isaac could only make out the sad rubble of spent bullet casings and empty suitcases and satchels, the litter of earth and plunder.

In the faint, straw glow of moonlight, he could make out a scraggly bush or two in the distance and some slender tufts of weed, but except these sparse signs of life, the landscape seemed barren.

Trying to stand, Isaac felt the sagging weight of the dead still pressing on him from above. No matter how hard he tried, he could not shake the feeling of still being in the grave. He tried to think of something else, anything, a single moment from the days before the war, but he could not manage one coherent thought. His senses just recorded the world about him mechanically. He could hear the rustling of a light wind, the cawing and screeching of distant birds, and he could smell the acrid odor of freshly turned earth, quicklime, and decay. But he could not feel anything, could not hold one thought, could not reason.

When he tried to walk, his body shook. Like an infant in the throes of a high fever, he felt every muscle and bone in his body shudder. He was abruptly and acutely aware of his nakedness for the first time, but felt no shame, no self-consciousness. It was just one more fact merely confirming he was alive.

A gust of wind blew ash and dirt against his skin and the chill of a midnight dampness made his teeth chatter. But he took one more step, and then another. He walked slowly, instinctively, recognizing nothing familiar, as if he had been dropped on the surface of some stark, lifeless planet. In his head, he was overwhelmed by the silence, and his memory filled with sounds of gunshots and cries. He wanted so much to turn and go back, toward the grave, toward his mother and father, to pull them into his arms and hold them tightly, saying goodbye over and over until he too died. But he kept on moving forward, not once glancing back.

Occasionally, he heard a distant sound of engines, but he ignored it. His pace quickened. As if in a daze, he fled from the memories behind him, stumbling forward. He didn't think about direction. He planned no journey. He was just walking, away from everything, toward the murkiness of a pale moonlit terrain.

For over an hour, he walked, falling from time to time over rocks or sudden gullies, or the pits and ruts of dirt roads. Then he stumbled from high rye grass onto a wide, cinder-covered path, and he realized where he was. This was a road he had traveled on before, many times, with his father. And he knew, just up ahead, there was a house.

Following the curve of the cinder road, he turned and, just as he remembered, there to the left was the outline of the house, its windows flickering faintly with the fire glow from a hearth. A thin spume of smoke trailed up from the chimney, turned and twisted by the light wind. It was the house he had expected, the home of Godtz, the dogcatcher.

He saw the shabby yard with the mangled wire fences and the dog sheds, nailed together crazily as if by a madman, with roofs slanting and walls angling this way and that. A dog could be heard howling; another seemed to whimper and bay like a sick wolf. There was no question about it. He was at Godtz's place.

Before he stepped a step closer, he had to think. Suddenly he was back in the world he had left days before. But nothing was dependable anymore. Even the most familiar landmark would have filled him with uneasiness. No one was reliable, no action was predictable. The image of the dog yard and the decrepit house reminded him of his own grotesqueness. He was numbly aware of his own nakedness, the garish wound across his eye, the dirt and clay mottling his body; he was no more than a corpse with lungs. His presence intruded upon the benign and implacable scene, his life a nettlesome reminder of the deadly war just beyond the borders. Isaac didn't belong anywhere.

For a moment, he thought of turning and going back to his family, but a bolder, more intense notion grew inside. A sharp surge of exhilaration left him breathless. He was, in spite of armies, ideologies and countries, still alive. In the face of hopelessness and anguish, his life was an undeniable fact. Though not fully conscious of the idea, nevertheless, Isaac's whole physical being was driven by the urge to continue living.

He wanted food, warmth, and clothing, and the house seemed irresistible, even though it belonged to the malevolent and savage Godtz. He could not resist the possibility of succor. So he started toward it.

When he reached the door, he hesitated. He was surrounded by the litter of dog scraps and refuse. All around him, just beyond the fences, he heard scratching, growling, a sudden fit of yelping dying away into a screech of pain. His own nakedness intensified his sympathy for the imprisoned animals. A fence creaked and rattled, a thud of body against chain and wire. Isaac grew uneasy. The sounds multiplied, each one startling Isaac more. He expected a large mastiff or doberman to appear at his back in an instant and leap with snarling jaws at his neck. Each new sound made him more fearful and more shameful of his vulnerability and nakedness.

Then he noticed a torn, soiled blanket flung over a woodpile and he quickly grabbed it, wrapping it about his shoulders and torso. It was short and meager, but it afforded Isaac some modesty and warmth. And he regained sufficient courage to knock.

First, he knocked gently against the yellowed pine door, splintered and gouged by claws and knives, as if an army of beasts and barbarians had stormed this portal over and over again. Then he knocked again, more insistently; this time he heard a clatter of movement inside, a low voice, then two gruff and harsh.

The door flung open. There was Godtz, holding a small lantern, dressed in a long, dark overcoat, with his unshaven face bristling with anger.

"What's this? What idiot...?"

Godtz stopped, surprised by the sight of this thin, short boy, mud-splattered, filthy and naked, clutching one of Godtz's own blankets around him.

"I need your help."

"Are you crazy? Chlop! Chlop! Get out of here!"

As the warmth of the house bathed over Isaac and the sparse, crude interior of the room beckoned to him like a palace, he thought quickly what to say. Chlop appeared, the giant hulking frame blocking Isaac's view for a moment. Chlop wore a tight wool cap, thick leather boots tied at the top with a twist of wire, and a brown jacket made of dogskins.

"What do you make of this, Chlop? He wakes us all up in the middle of the night. Stark naked, wearing my blanket! What do you think, Chlop? A thief, a madman?"

"It's me, Isaac. Lazar's boy."

"Maybe a killer," Godtz paused, touched the edge of the

soiled and tattered blanket Isaac wore, then rubbed the cheap fabric between his fingers as if it was fine silk.

Farther back in the house, Isaac caught sight of Godtz's daughter in a long, cotton housecoat with her hair drawn back into a tight bun. Her face appeared pasty and puffed, her eyes watery with sleep. But when she saw Isaac, she started to grin, then giggled with a breathless squeal. Isaac reddened with shame and tried to draw the blanket around his body even more tightly. In his haste, however, to cover his nakedness, the blanket slipped off his shoulders and fell to the ground. For a moment, Isaac stood completely naked again. Godtz's daughter screamed derisively, then turned away when her father glared back at her. She continued to laugh, gulping and gasping, while hiding her face from view. At that point, even Chlop started to leer at Isaac's scrawny body, increasing his mortification. But it passed quickly as soon as he covered himself again with the blanket.

At any other time in his life before, a moment like this would have been the worst nightmare he could ever conceive in all his youthful imaginings: to be mocked and ridiculed by a young woman while standing naked and helpless. But the feeling of shame and self-consciousness vanished quickly. He had no time for propriety or vanity. And as for shame, it was every-where, and everyone in Isaac's world deserved to feel it along with him.

"I was stripped and beaten by some soldiers on the way here," Isaac revealed in firm, convincing tones.

"I see. Just like that," Godtz sneered.

"It's true. My father is in hiding. He's alive and in good health, so help me. Novak, the owner of the movie theater, took my family in, but I was sent out to ask for help. Just some cloth-ing, food . . . . My father and mother are in hiding. They're safe."

Godtz peered and squinted at Isaac, trying to look right into the boy's head to find the truth. He chewed his lower lip tensely as he spoke. "I heard different. I heard all the Jews were killed in the Sosenki. Everyone heard the shooting. It went on for days. Your father, everyone, was killed. That's what I heard."

Isaac's mind raced ahead, desperately contriving new arguments to make his plea convincing. He knew as long as Godtz thought his father was alive, there were still debts, obligations, advantages and favors to be traded. He had never lied so blatantly before, and never with such bold conviction.

"My father wants you to know he is very much alive. In a few days, when the fighting moves on to the east, we'll all be back at the house and the factory will start up."

"So...," Godtz kept prying, "the rumors about the Sosenki, all the shooting we heard?"

"I don't know about any of that. I know my family is hiding and I was stripped and beaten by some soldiers. That's all I know."

"So, Chlop, what do you think? Our grimy little grub here wants a bit of help from us. What do you think?"

There was an undercurrent of nastiness in Godtz's voice, but Isaac couldn't determine whether it was just his normal tone of meanness and gruff manner, or a hint that he did not believe a word of Isaac's story.

Grabbing Chlop's arm, Godtz walked back into the darkness of the house to confer. For a moment, Isaac was alone once more, aware of the animal sounds all about him, the sweep of the wind rustling leaves and litter. He shivered and his knees ached with fatigue.

Suddenly Chlop appeared at the door, carrying a large bundle under his right arm. Without explanation, he put his left arm around Isaac and started to walk with him out to the side of the yard. In the bundle, Isaac could see a red shirt, a heel of bread, something like cheese. By the gate, Chlop indicated that

Isaac should take a drink from a large rain barrel. As Isaac nodded, scooping water up with one hand and splashing it into his face at first, he noticed Chlop move toward the corner of the house. As Isaac took another scoop of water from the barrel, Chlop started talking as he clumsily tried to conceal a long, thick wooden board behind his back.

"Godtz told me you should get dressed and eat and get some sleep. He wants to help." Chlop spoke tonelessly, without a trace of emotion.

But Isaac saw the board turning in Chlop's fist as the towering figure adjusted his grip on it. His hands were so big, he held the massive plank like it was a mere walking cane. Isaac quickly finished drinking and turned to face the hulking figure that approached, unsmiling, with his coarse jacket of matted dogskins, the weapon of wood clutched behind his back. Once again, Isaac felt the closeness of death, but he felt no fear; just a numb, impersonal kind of dread.

Dropping the board, to his side, and with it all his pretense about comfort and assistance, Chlop took Isaac by the back of his neck and pushed him toward the darkness beyond the fences. Somehow, the dogs, recognizing that their taskmaster Chlop was near, began to whimper and slink back into their tin and cardboard shelters.

But Isaac could not slink away. Chlop led him roughly to an open field by a dry culvert strewn with pebbles and weeds that ran past the house. There Chlop stopped, tightening the grip on Isaac's neck.

"Here is good." He swung the menacing board at his side freely now in the open. "Godtz said you're all dead anyway. This will make it easier for everyone, won't it?"

At that, Chlop pulled away Isaac's blanket, forced the boy to kneel and raised the piece of wood like a club above his head. Isaac saw everything happening at once. Chlop with his death blow, the moon growing transparent in the brightening dawn, his corpse tumbling down into the dry bed of the culvert and it all seemed familiar and inevitable. Then Isaac in the same crowded second felt the gold rings on his finger that his mother had given him just before the march. He had taken them for granted and, just now, in his clenched palm, he was aware of their shape, their feel. Touching them with his fingers, he was suddenly awakened with ideas and strategies again.

"Wait! Chlop! You mustn't. You know my family. My brother helped you when you were sick. We've always treated you well."

Isaac's fingers pressed down on the rings as if in their touch he could read some secret code, some kind of tender braille etched there by his mother. He knew exactly what to say as he rubbed the rings over and over in his palm. "Let me go and I'll be generous."

Chlop wavered above him. "Godtz said you had to be dead."

"I'll die anyway, Chlop. Just let me go. I promise you I'll die anyway. You can be sure of that. No one will ever see me again. You can tell Godtz you killed me and buried me. No one will ever know."

Chlop mumbled and rolled the thick piece of wood in his hand while the rings kept whispering through Isaac's fingers.

"I have gold right here. More gold than you will see in all your years. Two priceless rings. Heavy gold. See." He raised his hand and showed Chlop the rings. "See, feel them. Heavy gold." Then he quickly removed them and offered them to Chlop. "They're yours. Just don't kill me."

Chlop smiled as he held the rings in his hand. Then slowly, his demeanor changed. His face slackened, his body relaxed. He let the wood drop from his grip and he turned his back on Isaac to study the rings in the moonlight.

And Isaac kept talking, beseeching, as he kneeled, his arms clutched about this chest for warmth. "Who will know, Chlop?

It's our deal. And you will be rich as Godtz. Just like that. It's our deal."

When Chlop turned to face Isaac, he had decided. Lifting Isaac up, he took off his own jacket of dogskins and put it around Isaac's shoulders. Then he went toward the house, picked up the bundle of clothes and food, and brought it back, giving it abruptly to Isaac. "Go," he muttered.

It was happening so fast that Isaac could only nod and listen. He held the bundle tightly against his body, afraid that Chlop might change his mind again and take it back. But Chlop was finished thinking. He looked at the rings once more, smiled and turned away.

"Thank you," Isaac whispered, still stunned by the suddenness of Chlop's decision.

"I'm as rich as Godtz now, " Chlop concluded.

"Yes, that's for certain."

Chlop turned to face Isaac, his eyes brighter, fiercely alert. "I told you to go!" With that, Isaac started to run, down the culvert, up the other bank, cradling the bundle of food and clothing like a child. In the distance, he knew, stood the great expanse of the Volhynia woods, and beyond that, the marshes of Polessi. His heart was leaping at his chest, his lungs burned, but he kept running, sometimes bounding into the air with relief. Over and over again in his mind, he envisioned images of his mother and father. It was almost as if he was turning the pages of his family's photo album, each page more vivid and real than the next. He felt no pain, no fatigue now, and his dogskin jacket warmed him like a great overcoat of fine sable.

"Thank you," he whispered to his mother as he ran. Then "thank you" to his father and, as he spoke to them in his heart, he felt tears swelling up in both eyes. For the first time since he had climbed from his own grave, he could cry.

CHAPTER THREE
ISAAC, THE WOLF
ISAAC, THE BEAR

The forests of Volhynia cover a vast region in Poland, from the Carpathian foothills in the south to the alluvial marshlands of the Polessi Woods in the north. On the eastern border of Volhynia stand the steppes of Russia, and on the western border stretch the central lowlands of Lublin.

Centuries before Isaac, Volhynia had been the imperial hunting preserve of monarchs and noblemen. Its rich forests of birch, hazel, beech, elm and pine served to shelter the ancient Polish aristocrats from royal pretenders, usurpers, and conquerers.

When the great princes of the Jagiellonian Dynasty ruled, the silver-white and green hues of the forests glittered off the feathers of heathcocks and black storks, and off the backs of wild boar and roebucks. When King Casimir Jagiellon fought back the marauding Turks and Teutonic Knights, the dense woods concealed the endless caravans of soldiers and lords traveling to the wars; when the Tartars and Mongols threatened, it was under the vast pavilion of Volhynia's treetops that the exhausted warriors rested in jeweled and gilded tents, venturing out only to hunt the brown bear or woodcock.

For centuries the Volhynia would be carved up, partitioned, conquered and regained. But always it was a place of haughty, decadent retreat and leisure, far from the battleground and courtly intrigues.

Now it was Isaac's turn to escape to Volhynia. This son of a Rovno leather merchant slept in the arboreal splendor, wearing nothing but the bloodstained blouse and tattered shorts found inside Chlop's bundle, along with the dogskin jacket pulled tightly about his scrawny shoulders.

For the first days in the damp autumn mist, Isaac roamed about the woods aimlessly, frightened by his sudden and violent exile from country, kin and home. He was overwhelmed by the strangeness and vastness of this forest where he was neither lord nor invader, but rather an alien to all borders, a foreigner to earth itself.

At first Isaac tried to sleep at night, crouching beside the gnarled and bulging roots of the larger trees. But at night between the echoing pillars of elms and pines, the sounds of animal life and wind blended into a steady, unnerving moan. He was startled by every crackle of twig, every howl and baleful gust. Once, he was sure he heard the baying of distant wolves and remembered the legions of stories he had heard from his aunt about the steppes of Russia with its roving packs of wolves. He recalled her description of one poor village's ordeal when the wolves descended in the middle of a fierce winter to devour horses and babies alike, hurtling through windows, crunching through wooden cradles and bolted doors to snare bawling babies in their jaws. With such thoughts, Isaac slept fitfully, rising with every screech, every growl and creak.

He would try to dig with his fingers down between the roots of the tree, burrowing out a small cavity for his body, and in that shallow well, surrounded by the harboring arms of the roots, Isaac felt safer. He was in his own lair, a mother's lap made up of mulched leaves and scaly bark. By the third night, he had learned to cover himself with a blanket of loose leaves and branches.

But on a morning near the end of the first week, Isaac awoke to face a pelting ice storm that covered his body with a coating of heavy sleet. He learned from that morning to pick the side of a tree carefully before sleeping, to check the wind's direction, attempting in the future to use each tree as a wall against storms and northern winds.

But if night was a long, dark ordeal, daytime was even more frightening. It wasn't the sound of wild beasts or the lash of fierce storms he feared in the day; it was the presence of other human beings. If he heard the rusty creak of a wagon wheel or the distant clamor of voices, Isaac would panic. Every accent, each inflection, whether Polish, German, Ukrainian or Lithuanian, was a curse set against him. If he saw a clearing or a meadow, a tilled field or a rick of newly mown hay, Isaac would retreat. If a distant farmhouse came into view, he would recoil and run back into a grove or thicket. He could not bear the thought of encountering another human being.

During the day, especially, he felt like an easy target, too visible and too vulnerable. And deep inside his once loving and trusting soul, he felt the gnawing of hate and suspicion. Sometimes he even felt guilty that he was alive, that his presence in these woods was a mistake, a miscalculation by the gods. It was only right he should be stalked and hunted down like some wild quarry, then driven back to the burial pit and executed once again, properly and finally.

On the sixth day of his survival, with a wail of blinding sleet falling, he accidentally stumbled across a road and heard the sound of a horse-drawn cart not more than a few feet away hidden by the gray screen of ice. Isaac couldn't tell from which direction the voices came so he just stood for a moment, paralyzed with fear, then fell to the ground by the side of the road, flattening himself out in a shallow ditch, and held his breath.

The cart with Polish-speaking occupants passed above him, the voices rumbling as loudly as the wooden wheels which passed inches from Isaac's trembling body. The two were talking about the Germans' rewards for their "enemies."

"For one of them, captured alive, it's just a sack of salt!"

"No! Two sacks! For a live one, one salt and one sugar. If it's a dead one you find, it's just a sack of salt."

"Who cares? No matter. Stay out of it all, I say. Salt. Sugar. No matter. Keep your mouth shut. You're better off."

"But a sack of sugar. Think of it."

"Look at you! Your eyes are covered with icicles, your mouth is nearly frozen stiff and you keep talking about sugar. Stop dreaming! Don't be an onion head. Stay out of it all!"

Isaac thought, *Salt, sugar . . . for what . . . for who?* He swallowed hard and clutched the icy dirt as the cart pulled away into the gray mist of sleet. *For who? A dead Jew? A live Jew? How much am I worth,* Isaac pondered sadly. *A pinch of salt? With my skin and bones? A cupful of sugar?* But then he remembered his family's neighbor, the fireman, charging in, bartering for the furniture before his family was even taken. *A cupful of sugar would be enough incentive. It would be worth their while to turn me in.* He quickly rose and disappeared back into the dense forest.

The next day, still frozen wet, Isaac discovered the body of a German soldier by a small creek. His pants and boots were missing, and his gray Wehrmacht jacket had been ripped to shreds by bullet holes. Unthinkingly, Isaac approached the body and touched it with his foot. For shoes, Isaac wore only cloth strips wound about his ankles and toes like primitive moccasins. Through them, he could feel the clammy stiffness of the soldier's body. He pushed the body again, almost expecting a response; but of course, there was no movement. Then, as if a valve inside Isaac's soul exploded open, he began kicking even harder; once, twice. With his third kick, he jammed his cold heel into the chest of the soldier. At that moment even greater rage and vengeance erupted inside of him and he fell upon the corpse, pounding it with his fist, screaming and crying, his body shaking, his anger and fury unchecked and unbridled for the first time in his life.

For a moment it seemed like Isaac wouldn't stop until he had bludgeoned and crushed the soldier's body into the rocks by the icy stream, but just as abruptly as he had exploded, he suddenly quieted. Exhausted, spent, he knelt by the corpse, still shaking, his chest heaving, his breath coming in gasps and sobs.

For many minutes he knelt by the body; then, catching his breath and gathering his strength once more, he turned to the dead body only as an object to be used. He touched the jacket, but was repelled by the jagged bullet holes, the thick cloth threads twisted in with flesh and caked with blood. Spotting matches in the vest pocket, he quickly took the pack and rushed off, up the embankment and into the forest once more.

With matches, he thought, he could build a fire; he could warm and dry himself, he could cook meat or soup. His father taught him years ago that even poison ivy once boiled is not only safe but an endless source of iron and strength. With fire he could not only survive, he could thrive.

But, of course, he was not thinking it through. After gathering kindling wood, he sat down at dusk to light his first fire. As he put the lit match up to the thin twigs, the flicker of flames and the curling spout of smoke reminded him of danger. The smoke from any fire would soon rise above the trees and be spotted, while the flames could be seen for miles as a revealing gleam in the woods. There must not be any fire, Isaac realized. Not if he wished to remain concealed, not if he wished to live. He quickly shoveled dirt on the crackling twigs and smothered the flame. It would be the last fire he would sit beside for eight months.

Even by the end of the first week, he was still eating the bread and cheese Chlop had given him. He had guarded them with care and nibbled at them with the frugality of a mouse. Then the dogskin jacket with its untreated and uncured skin began to stink. A rank odor of decay from the skins filled Isaac's nostrils, but he clung to the jacket for warmth and protection. With the stench came disintegration. During one night of sleep, the poor stitching rotted away and by the morning, the jacket had literally dissolved off Isaac's back, decomposing into scattered patches of yellowish hide. It was as if he had molted in the night, casting away old skin, sloughing off dead scales.

Isaac awoke colder than ever. The wind had shifted in the night and had come around the southeast, blowing away his blanket of leaves and branches and with it some of the remains of his dogskin jacket.

It was during that night that he had one of his recurring dreams. He tried not to dwell on them in the daylight for they disturbed him with odd, terrifying flashes of memory. Images from his past would always jolt him from sleep with his heart racing and his head aching from grief.

The dreams were always of objects of vague faceless images as if someone had gone through Isaac's family album and cropped off the heads of all the pictures. Often he dreamt of his grandfather's cane, abandoned by his bed. It would suddenly leap to life and dance about as if some invisible puppeteer controlled it, jerking and tugging it by a hidden string. The cane would first bang harmlessly against the bedpost, then smash into the chairs and the dresser. Finally, in an increasing frenzy of destruction, the cane would shatter windows and poke holes through the walls as if it was trying to escape. The clatter and clamor of destruction would ring in Isaac's ears long after he had awakened.

Some nights he would dream of his father's wagon standing empty in a field on a hot, sunny day. When he looked inside, he'd recognize his parents' finest clothing strewn about on the floor of the wagon. Isaac would climb onto the buckboard and try to make the horse move, but it wouldn't respond. Even when he lashed the reins across its back, it stood still as stone. Nothing moved. It was then he'd feel the hard, bony tap of a finger on his shoulder. Then another sharp tap on the other shoulder. Isaac knew with a shudder that his parents were behind him, but he also knew he must not turn around. He'd continue to feel the jab of fingers on his back and each time he fought the impulse to turn around. And that's how he awoke, his mind still trapped in that immobile wagon, frozen between the wrenching nightmare of the recent past and the unspoken terror of each new day.

By the beginning of the second week in the Volhynia region, Isaac began to deal with the realities. He knew he could not wander aimlessly about from day to day, shrinking from every sound, hiding in every ditch and gully from the voices and animals. He knew that his only hope would be to travel north to the swamps of Pinsk and Pripet in the Polessi woods. His father had warned him that no one dared to venture into those northern marshes, but he also taught his son how to survive in such a place.

However, there was practically nothing left from the bundle Isaac had clutched entering these woods. He had to improvise, and soon, if he was not to starve or freeze to death.

It was during the second week that Isaac decided he would have to travel at night and sleep during the day. In that way, he was convinced he could make more progress, traveling farther and freer without concern for visibility. He would have to become nocturnal.

He also realized he would have to eat from the bounty of the forest, eating what his father had taught him was safe, like the whitest, unspeckled mushrooms only, and the broadleaf grass that was lined like the palm of a man's hand. He remembered so much of his father's advice on those picnics in the Sosenki, advice about watching the animals and eating only what they eat, and touching only what they touch.

So Isaac began to travel at night during the second week, sleeping through the daylight and eating off the forest floor.

He discovered that hiding in a poorly dug cavity between the roots of trees was not enough. During the day he could be too easily discovered, so he decided to climb certain trees and make a sleeping pallet out of intertwined twigs and boughs. By the end of that second week, he was traveling many miles north through the night and sleeping by day in the tops of Volhynia trees.

A sudden warm spell just before winter took his mind off clothing for a moment and he could focus on food. The first week of this new routine brought him a carefully picked collection of white, unmottled mushrooms, along with clumps of grass deemed edible by his father. He would even pull off the barks of some trees for eating if he saw the claw marks of some bear gouged into the trunk or bits of wood bitten off.

When he came across a harvested field of cabbages, he discovered that cabbage stems were unaccountably cut off, discarded and plowed under. Isaac would wait until dark and then sneak into the fields. Going from furrow to furrow, he dug up the buried cabbage stems, usually with the help of some jagged metal scrap picked up near a bomb crater or a demolished vehicle. These cabbage stems lasted longer than any other food and tasted best of all. Alhough, now again, Isaac did chip a tooth biting into the spiked root of the plant.

During the warm weather, Isaac discovered another source of food—the roadside shrine. The shrines were simply built, just a base of stones and pebbles topped with a crude plaster form of the Madonna or Jesus about a foot high, with an arching roof of pine bough and leafy thatch to protect the sacred statue from the elements.

Farmers and merchants, carting or hauling their produce to the nearby market in town, would pause at these roadside shrines and leave a reverent token of their harvest at the foot of the sacred statue.

The local residents set out for the market early in the morning and passed the shrines before the sun rose. It was in this early morning shadow that Isaac would hide and watch as each grateful traveler knelt with an armful of fruits and vegetables as offering. They were usually the most bruised and overripe of the produce—tomatoes with pulpy blemishes, soft mottled apples, spoiled potatoes, and onions, blotchy and soft. But Isaac didn't mind. He would wait in the bushes nearby until the wagons passed, then rush out, scoop up as much of the produce as he could, then fly back to the forest.

In the comfort and safety of the Volhynia woods, Isaac fed on holy offerings. Their imperfections were ideal for Isaac's teeth and stomach, soft enough to be chewed without chipping any more teeth, overripe enough to be digested with little effort. The roadside shrine was a godsend. Until the snow drifted over the plaster altars, Isaac would go out of his way to find these shrines, waiting in the early morning darkness behind the trees. He could feast for days off the harvest from one of these shrines.

He learned to observe everything more carefully now that he could only move in the night. In time his eyesight and hearing would develop and sharpen until he was able to see and hear at night as well as he had in the day.

Adapting to this new routine, Isaac learned to grow accustomed to the cadences of animals and forest noises. Soon he was able to sit comfortably in the fork of an elevated bough, nibbling on a handful of sour grass or on a glaringly white mushroom.

He found that he slept more peacefully in the day, in his precarious perch high in the trees. Somehow, being removed from the earth, suspended in sleep and dream above the roads and the ditches and the voices, gave Isaac a sense of transcendence. He slept beyond the pull of gravity and war, above the snares and traps of countrymen, and out of reach from the jaws of wolves and the swipe of bears.

In this new lifestyle of survival, he also learned how to store his food. In his foraging about, he discovered a discarded postal bag stenciled with the name of a nearby town. It had been left in the midst of war rubble near a demolished wagon, surrounded by a spill of shell casings and jagged shards of shrapnel. The letters and packages that might have been in the cloth bag had either blown away or been stolen. This ample, sturdy bag became Isaac's portable larder that he hauled on his back. In it, he shoved grass, mushrooms, nuts, and bark—anything that seemed edible to him or the animals. Only the grass would not benefit from such storage, perishing quickly, withering into a brown, dry pile of friable husks.

With the food on his back, Isaac could now face the increasing chill and the winter of ice. He needed clothing—layers of it—to stay warm. He would first prowl about at night looking for an isolated farmhouse, far from villages and large roads. Then, in the dark of night, Isaac would crawl slowly towards the house, always keeping an eye out for dogs, stray hunters, and the inevitable white flash of sheets from a clothesline.

Since most dogs by this time of the war had been roped up by their masters so that rambunctious soldiers and partisans would not shoot them for sport or food, Isaac only worried about the length of rope and the distance to the clothesline.

The first night he tried to steal clothing and sheets, he

crossed a wide, open pasture. Luckily, it was a dark night with a sliver of moon barely illuminating this silent, stealthy individual slipping like a lynx toward the house.

Near the half-collapsed chicken coop, Isaac saw the clothesline, full of underwear, sheets, even a long housecoat he could strip into moccasins. Carefully circling about the clucking and scratching chickens, he reached the line without a problem. But just as he grabbed for some garments and folded the long sheet under his arm, he heard a growl, then a sharp, angry bark. Isaac turned but did not see the dog. Another bark followed. The beast seemed almost upon him. Clutching what he had grabbed, Isaac started to run blindly toward the field. He did not see the dog's tethered rope stretched taut in front of him, so he tripped over it with a sprawling thud, releasing underwear, cotton slips, housecoats, and sheets to the ground. For a moment he felt lightheaded, the fall knocking the wind out of him. But then he heard a new noise, from the house, and a gleam from a newly lit lantern beamed out onto the field. Isaac panicked. He grabbed the sheet and started to scramble away. But the sheet didn't go with him. At the other end, holding on to one corner of the white cloth were the bolt-like jaws of a squat, brown mastiff, muttering and snarling while it anchored the sheet. Isaac tugged once again, but the sheet did not leave the dog's mouth. Instead, the dog pulled back with a jerk of his head and Isaac stumbled backwards. The mastiff could not venture farther, having extended his rope to its limits, but he held one end of the sheet with the ferocity of a lamprey eel. The farmer could be heard shouting in the distance. More lights spilled out of the windows onto the fields. In desperation, Isaac managed one more wrenching tug on the sheet. It tore at the edges near the dog's teeth and the rest of the sheet pulled free. With that Isaac leaped into the air with joy and sped quickly toward the trees, waving the torn sheet in the air like a captured flag.

Some nights, as he grew bolder, he'd misjudge the location of a farmhouse, seeing only the lure of flashing sheets and fluttering underwear. Not realizing how close the house was to a village or to a main road, he would find himself close to a military convoy or a crowd of villagers, and barely escape. Other nights he would come too close to a tethered dog and manage to flee with only a gouge of skin torn off an ankle or wrist.

Through all the mishaps, he managed to make progress toward the north, night after night. The trees grew shorter and sparser, the ground spongier even in the increasing freeze of winter. The marshlands were approaching after a month of wandering. By now, as he crossed the provincial border into the Polessi region, he was dressed in a motley array: underwear from some pig farmer, a blouse from a miller, a long, brown military coat stolen off the corpse of a Russian soldier by a Polish merchant that Isaac stole in turn off the merchant's porch.

Isaac would pick his farmhouse targets even more carefully now, wrapping his hands and forearms with thick cloth to ward off the attacking dogs. Often, he would club a dog back so hard with his padded arm, the animal would stumble backward from the blow, then turn tail and run, yelping and whining back to its hutch. The rumor among local farmers and merchants near the border was that a pack of wolves had been driven by the German invasion from the steppes into Russian territory, observing no sovereignty but hunger. It was these wolves that terrorized their clotheslines and their dogs.

Early one morning, just after Isaac had found a tall, sturdy tree to climb and a thick web of boughs to sleep upon, he noticed movement in the distant bushes. Holding his breath as he hugged the heavy branch for support, Isaac watched from the height of the tree as a large brown bear approached. It reared upon its hind legs and swayed menacingly with its paws outstretched in the air, then back on all fours, lumbering forward with a rippling step toward a tree adjacent to Isaac's. Hulking upward to a standing position once again, the bear began to claw at the bark with one paw while hugging the trunk with the other. After a moment of scratching, he would start to lick at the bark; his tongue, thick and slobbering, slapped at the trunk. Then the bear would begin clawing again, followed once more by a luxurious lapping at the second bark. Isaac watched it all in awe, respectful of the bear's power and suppleness. He envied the brown fur, bristling and glistening in the winter breeze. Each time the bear would begin to slather at the wet bark, he would exhale cloudy vapors that would condense in the air and circulate about his ears. He was like some supple, thick-furred god with his head in self-made clouds, absorbed totally in his task, while Isaac watched worshipfully.

When the bear finally left, Isaac quickly descended and approached the bear's tree. There, in the grooves cut by the fierce claws, Isaac saw the ooze of sap, viscous and honey-colored. With a hesitant gesture, he ran his fingers over the syrupy flow and put it in his mouth. It tasted strange, neither tart nor unctuously sweet, almost pleasant. Again and again, in the brightening yellow light of the sunrise, Isaac ran his fingers over the clawed bark, scooping the syrup with the same methodicalness as the bear. After a few minutes, he felt satisfied, sated on the honey of the cloud-crowned beast, and returned to his rest high in the trees.

By the end of November, Isaac was well into the region of marshes and swamps. Aware of the treachery of the land, he maneuvered carefully, jumping from one grassy tuft of island to another, avoiding the spongy ice-crusted depth of watery pits that seemed deceptively solid and overgrown with sedge and reeds. During the night, Isaac would attempt to move off the marshes into the thin, sparse woods of Polessi to forage, but the winter was setting in and it was becoming more difficult to find clothes and food.

One evening, Isaac woke to a swirling snow storm. Huddled by a squat pine tree, hidden by foliage and branches, Isaac was still covered with snow, spitting it out of his mouth, wiping it from his eyes and nose. Everything was covered white. The land had sunk beneath this chilling mantle. He would have to depend more and more on his postal bag—his cloth larder—and eat sparingly. But with the diminished access to food, his strength began to sap and he was forced to drag the postal bag behind him, unable to bear the slight weight on his back.

With his body weakening, the cold penetrated deep into his marrow. Some mornings, no matter how much he wore, his elbows and knees seemed frozen and his skin grew drier and icier. He fell asleep one day for so long that he forgot his routine and didn't wake until the following morning. He could barely move under the weight of fatigue and cold. But he was too worn and weak to venture forth. He envied the beavers he had watched, building their winter dams in the warmth of an understream, and he prayed for some kind of miracle to bring the spring sun early. For days, he stopped moving and just dug in the snow, rooting like a squirrel, for bits of kernels and nuts.

Nearing the end of his larder one day late in December, three months into his solitary exile and survival, he went to sleep shivering and shaking like he had some awful fever. He dreamt of oranges and hot meadows, whirring with insects and birds; he saw distant fires burning on hillsides just beyond his village and tried to run toward their warmth. When he awoke, it was twilight. There was still the thick crust of snow across the land, but he felt warmer somehow. Perhaps a fever. But when he stood up, he realized how strange his own body felt. Unbuttoning his blouse, peering down into the two night shirts he had stolen months before, he saw great shags of hair on his chest. Feeling the rest of his arms and back as best he could, he felt hair everywhere. Not just short bristles accompanying manhood, or the soft down of puberty, but thick matted hair, like the fur of the bear. It covered his chest, his back, his arms. He could feel it thick against his pants and down his legs. He was astounded, even a bit frightened at first, but the newfound warmth that the sudden sprouting of hair provided left him stronger. He was sure it was some sign. He was given a new boon, a new shield, to fight off the winter. Just like the wolf and the bear, he knew he would survive this season as well.

CHAPTER FOUR
SERGEI AND THE BARBARIANS

It was so easy to sleep. Isaac huddled in the coarse sedge, his hands and feet tangled in the reeds, his head resting on ice-crusted thatch, and there he would dream of wandering through the streets of Rovno.

After eight months of hiding, first in the woods of Volhynia and now in the swamps of the Polessi, Isaac had grown weak and gaunt. Though the northern marshes had provided him with the safety and concealment he had sought during these harsh months of winter, Isaac had stopped caring. He stopped worrying about the whiteness of mushrooms or the seclusion of farmhouses. He had even grown careless crossing the swamps.

No villager or soldier dared enter the watery heart of the Polessi. In order to traverse it safely, you had to leap deliberately from one outcropping of dry land to another. Each rise of firm land was just slightly elevated above the water level and deceptively hidden by stunted trees and scraggly bushes. Between these dry places lay the watery sloughs of treacherous and snagging roots. For a time Isaac had moved confidently and quickly through this landscape, his footing and bearing always certain and safe. But lately he had grown reckless.

After eight months of hiding, without speaking one word to another human being or touching another hand or shoulder, Isaac found himself slipping away from reality. As he physically weakened, he was increasingly unable to associate the young romantic boy of his dreams with the body he now inhabited, covered with stiff, mud-caked garments and that beastly bristle of body hair carpeting his skin. In his dreams, Isaac was still smooth-skinned and brightly dressed, bounding along in the sparkle of a Rovno afternoon. His dream image was nothing like the creature he had become, cowering in the shadow of reeds and high grass during the daylight, prowling through the night like some fugitive beast. This nocturnal swamp figure, scrambling from one clump of dry underbrush to another, belonged to a region of existence that Isaac had never visited in memories or dreams.

With his body shriveling to a mere fifty pounds and his vitality sapped, he had begun to travel in circles. Leaping across the bottomless fens of the Polessi marshes, he imagined his body nothing more than a parched and aching husk. It didn't matter to him in these last weeks whether he tread on dry land or sank into the mud. Once, he leaped weakly towards what appeared to be a firm, dry elevation of land, only to plunge unexpectedly into the muck and swirl of the swamp. Instead of fighting and thrashing against the pull of the muddy vines and entangling reeds, he relented and let the feeble freight of his body sink.

For a moment he went under, engulfed by the cloudy ooze of the quagmire. He allowed the mud to take grip of his feet, sucking him down slowly into the maw of the swamp. He had the sensation of floating upside down, sideways, with no sense of sky or land, east or west; but such sudden and utter loss of direction and bearing just as quickly caused panic in his mind. And he began to grapple and splash about. Shaken from the fleeting and near-fatal lethargy, he grabbed hold of a long, sinuous root and pulled himself towards some narrow bank of dry land.

Too exhausted to eat, too weak to walk, Isaac slept after these desperate seconds through the night into the next day, awakening only to gnaw sluggishly on some splotchy mushroom or on a handful of torn grass, then falling back to sleep once again. His dreams had grown more and more enticing, enveloping him as surely as the boggy waters of the swamp.

He would dream about the boyhood streets of Rovno and he would walk those roads once again in dream: Skolkia Street, Pantowksi Way, Woylia Road. Every inch and corner were vividly familiar, but in his slumber, the streets were always empty and the houses seemingly deserted.

On Skolkia Street, he recognized the dark gray sandstone of his old schoolhouse. Behind the arched windows, he imagined the sweet, doleful eyes of Morris grinning in the shadows behind the arched window; then between the ionic columns of the main entrance, he thought he saw the lanky, awkward form of Hagar. But they both vanished and he was alone, completely, in his beloved town.

Every house appeared perfect, glittering with a fresh coat of paint or plaster; the ornamented peaked roofs and miniature cupolas radiated in the sunlight. Just beyond Woylia Road, Isaac saw Gochov Synagogue rising before him with its glowing stained-glass window. But inside he saw no one, heard no chanting, and only noticed the pale beam of light breaking through the great window and beaming down into the corner of the temple. There was nothing but gray dust and shadows inside.

Nonetheless, even in the middle of a deserted Rovno, Isaac felt warm and sheltered. Everything was so familiar, so vivid and sharp. He could even smell the sweet stickiness of the pine forest and the faint, acrid odor of curing leather. Then, sweeping away all other scents and aromas, the pungent and savory tang of his mother's stew asserted itself.

At that point in his dreams, he often heard a giggle, and saw the loping stride of Hagar as he vanished into an alley, his long legs pumping awkwardly like a sprinting stork. A face or two would appear at some Gothic window and scatter into broken shafts of light. Then Isaac saw the distant millstones of the leather factory as though it was right in front of him, and by it, his brother's clinic with its white roof pure and luminous under the bright sky.

If the smell of the stew and the sight of his homestead did not drive him longingly into consciousness, Godtz's daughter would.

Suddenly he was in the market square by the public fountain with its Polish crest at the center, spouting water.

He always remembered the gypsies, with their bulky garb and gaudy colors, using this fountain, as if they were carrying all their wardrobe and furnishings under one patchwork coat. They would come to the fountain carrying cracked yellowing pots and pitchers. But by the fountain in this dream stood Godtz's daughter. She leaned over the lip of the basin, absolutely naked, beckoning to Isaac to take her in his arms. There she stood, as he once stood in front of her. And he saw her, as with every other detail in these images, sharply and distinctly. In high relief, with perspectives foreshortened and sharp, he saw her by the fountain with her breasts, full and pink, her thighs shadowy and rough, and her thick midriff smooth and pale. Over her entire body he could not help but see a brown dusting of hair like some hazy veil. Fascinated and embarrassed, Isaac turned away and then heard her laughter slice through him. She would erupt into a watery gurgle of a laugh that grew so shrill, it drove Isaac back into reality. He would awake in astonishment in the midst of brush and swamp, buffeted by the icy shear of the wind and the cold grizzly look of the desolate terrain.

By the beginning of May, Isaac could barely drag himself into the sparse woods surrounding the swamp. He had grown so weak, he was unable to negotiate the watery sloughs of the marshes, and he chose the dry land permanently. It didn't bother him there was little cover and that activity in nearby towns would surely spill over into his vicinity. He could only walk a few hours now, and then he would collapse. His body sagged beneath the weight of patchwork coats he had fashioned out of bedsheets, blankets and coarse underwear, along with the linen wrappings about his arms and legs.

He would collapse not far from a road, hidden only by the dip of a shallow ravine or a low-slung shrub. But he made no effort to move or hide. It didn't matter to him. He was unable to breathe. If he tried to lift himself into a kneeling position, he would break into a coughing fit and fall into a sprawling heap once more. There he would stay, trying to sleep once more, his breathing shallow and labored, his movements painful and slight. He desired sleep more than anything and would hope this time he would never awake from the sight of the pure and holy Rovno of his dreams.

On the fifth day of May, after eight months of exile from his childhood world, Isaac realized he could not muster sufficient energy to travel ever again. Near a hazel grove on this shale-gray, overcast day, Isaac lay down. He was too weak to swallow and too befuddled to even find some kind of food. So he stretched out not far from a main road and let the thawing warmth of a May breeze lull him into deep, inexhaustible sleep. His dream was of Rovno once more. But this time the streets were crowded and noisy. People went by Isaac, jostling him with their shoulders, pushing and shoving him back towards the walls of the houses. He recognized the market sounds, the merchant's pitch and fast tempo, the shrill gossip of neighbors. The voices crowded around him in the darkening streets, and then he heard even harsher voices, above his head. The faces about him passed in a blur. In the distance, however, he could make out his father, standing by his wagon. Oddly, his father was dressed in his Great War uniform and stood very still.

A voice, very close and very insistent, broke through Isaac's concentration.

"I want those boots, Pietka! Now!"

Then another voice responded, softer and relenting, "What do I do, Stepan? Go barefoot?"

These voices were clearer and closer than any in the buzz and din of the Rovno marketplace. Then his father's face drew closer, growing larger before his eyes. It was the face Isaac remembered from the family photo album taken when Lazar was a prisoner of war in Austria. Like a grainy, faded vision, Lazar loomed before Isaac, crowding out all sight of Rovno. And in this photographic stillness he heard his father speak, "When God calls, always say yes . . . Always volunteer. Do business with Barbarians. Business is business even with Barbarians. Do business with them. Do. Do."

Isaac woke suddenly, startled by his father's voice and all-encompassing image. His father's message still echoed in his ears, while just beyond where Isaac rested, unfamiliar voices could be heard. Now a Polish accent, then a Ukrainian and even Russian now and then, in short and explosive exchanges.

"Novak, did you hear something?" A mellow Polish accent was clear, lighthearted, relaxed.

"Shut up! You and your ears." The reply was in a gruff, impatient Ukrainian accent.

Then a Russian voice cried out, "I hear it, too!"

Isaac did not move and he tried to hold his breath. Inside his head, his father's voice persisted, "Do business . . . with Barbarians . . . Business is business . . . Do . . . Do!"

He tried to turn over on his stomach silently, but rolled over some dry brush, snapping twigs and breaking his cover.

"Who's there!"

"In the bushes . . ."

"I'll kill him." The aggressive Ukrainian accent exploded. "Get him out of there. I'll kill him."

Isaac gripped the earth, breathlessly terrified, and yet somehow relieved. Even if he wanted to, he could not run away. He could not fight. He was barely able to stand.

"Now! Show yourself! We're waiting!"

He tried to crawl away, but his own arms were rubbery and numb. Then he went short of breath and gasped, breaking into a coughing fit. It was a helpless situation.

"Yes . . . yes. I see him!" Through his coughing, he heard the snap and click of gun bolts locking. It was all over. After eight months, it would finally end.

Isaac stood up, slowly, wavering. His swollen joints flared with pain, his body trembled as he coughed. The men scattered for cover, keeping their rifles and pistols trained on this target from behind the bushes, a short, cadaverously thin boy dressed in heaps of garments, layer upon layer of shreds and pieces.

Isaac looked about him, too weak, too confused to say anything. He saw at least six or seven men, all dressed differently. Some were in Russian uniforms with cartridge belts cinching peasant blouses; some wore parts of German uniforms—a Wehrmacht jacket here, an officer's cap over there. Some wore nothing military, but simply overalls and a heavy coat. This was no army; this was not even a band of dedicated partisans, committed to ideals and political goals. This was a ragtag group, as Isaac soon learned, made up of Ukrainian army deserters who fled conscription by the Germans; Russian prisoners, escaping deportation by the SS; and Polish citizens, driven from their homes by the horror of war. They had no convictions in common, except one—to stay out of the war. That meant staying alive in the forests by foraging, plundering, and guile. Sometimes it meant killing even an innocent witness like Isaac, so that their location would never be traced.

Stepan, the rough Ukrainian deserter, stepped forward. He was the most powerful of them, built like a circus strongman, with monumentally square shoulders, bulging forearms and a vast iron-ribbed chest. He was armed with every type of weapon from leg to arm. Bandoliers of bullets criss-crossed his shirt, holsters hung from inside his vest, sheaths of knives of all sizes were tied to arms and legs. He was a walking arsenal, dauntless and reckless in his aggressiveness.

"He's a piece of crap. A boy. Nothing. Just garbage." With that, Stepan removed a thin, serrated hunting knife from a sheath tied by leather thongs to his thigh. Holding the gleaming, angry knife aloft, he announced, "I'll do him a favor and cut his throat."

Isaac did not flinch. He was terrified, but also humiliated. There was nothing he could possibly do but submit. His eyes welled with tears, and his breathing grew even more labored and shallow. But just as Stepan stomped towards him with the knife, another man, younger and gentler looking, called Pietka, stepped forward, blocking Stepan's way. He stood with his back to the strong man, facing Isaac, and whispered, "I know you. Your brother saved my sister from the pox. I saw you at his clinic in Rovno. Tell them you're a doctor. Are you listening?"

Isaac looked at the pleasant face. He was a Polish mechanic from Rovno with a small thick nose and puckish grin.

Pietka tried again, "Tell them you're Russian . . . . Make up a name. Any name. You can help us with medicine. Tell them, damn it!"

Stepan grabbed Pietka by the shoulder. "What's this runt to you? He's a disease, garbage. We can't drag him along with us."

"Stepan, you fool. Didn't you hear what he said?"

Pietka glanced pleadingly at Isaac, trying to salvage his life. "He's a medical student . . . from Kiev. That's what he says. His name is Sergioski and he studied medicine. We could use him.

Are you listening, Stepan?"

Stepan paused, waited for Isaac to say something, then with renewed purpose, he flung Pietka aside. "He's garbage we should bury." The other men just watched, anxiously glancing about in case some other military convoy or police vehicle came into sight. One of them, another Pole called Novak, whispered out loud in a hoarse, anxious voice, "We can't stay out in the open like this. It's practically broad daylight. We have to move!"

"In a second," Stepan reassured, grabbing Isaac by the ragged collar of his patch work coat. "You're half-dead already, runt!"

Pietka cried out, futilely, "Stepan, he's no danger to us. What are you doing?"

With knife posed to slice across Isaac's neck, Stepan shoved his fist under Isaac's chin. It was at this very moment before his execution that Isaac truly understood his father's message in the vision of his face.

"Kill me." Isaac blurted it out, almost defiantly. "You're right, I'm nothing. Kill me."

"What?" Stepan was startled by Isaac's frank challenge. This skeleton of a boy dressed like a dingy and disgusting gypsy was exhorting Stepan to murder. The strong man was confused by the absence of fear and cowardice. Isaac glanced at Pietka, almost nodding, but without once changing his sullen, set expression.

"I'm no g...good to you," Isaac admitted. The sentences were difficult to form. He had not conversed with anyone for eight months and it was an effort to talk. He stumbled, spitting out each word with difficulty. "I can...only...coo...co ok a little, sew maybe...and do...do some surgery. Remove b...bu...bullets, close wounds, fi...fix bones...maybe. I'm no use to anyone. Do you think...?"

Pietka started to grin broadly. "See, I told you. Do you hear,

Stepan. Dumb!! . . . Do you hear?"

"He's no doctor. Don't hand me that." Stepan was persistent, anxious to finish off his quarry.

"Then kill me. I was . . . a Russian student in Kiev, and I was on my way to Lybov for further study. But I'm no doctor. I just know a little . . . about medicine, sickness . . . just a little."

Pietka was relishing every moment of Isaac's deception. Stepan lowered his knife.

Pietka rushed in, "I told you, you boob! A Russian medical student . . . called Sergioski, but we'll call him Sergei . . . Is that all right?" Pietka inquired of Isaac as he moved to the befuddled Stepan. "Put that knife away, Stepan. You could kill someone with that knife. Right, Sergei?" Isaac nodded weakly and smiled back at Pieta. Stepan turned away, growling and disheartened. "I want your boots, Pietka. Soon!"

With Stepan withdrawing from his attack, the other men felt emboldened enough to walk up to Isaac and help. No one asked any questions, not even Pietka who knew more than anyone about what brought Isaac to this wilderness.

Wasic, the other Polish member, shook Isaac's hand vigorously, almost toppling the boy to the ground. Novak, a Russian from the borders of Lithuania, loosened the harness of one of the two German Mannlicher rifles he was carrying and offered it to Isaac. He thrust it proudly into the boy's gut, but the weight of the weapon was too much and Isaac stumbled backwards a few feet. His strength had vanished from every muscle in his body. He could not grip the rifle or even hug it to his body. It slipped through his grasp like his arms were made of jelly. Novak was stunned by Isaac's feebleness, and Pietka laughed it off. "What he needs is a few extra muscles from Stepan." There was some laughter and Pietka picked up the Mannlicher and quietly hooked the harness strap around Isaac's hand.

As they started off into the denser woods and the higher

elevation, Stepan led the way. Pietka stayed back with Isaac, conversing in whispers in the Polish dialect of Rovno. Both young men had common bonds—their town, their schooling, a legendary doctor. But Pietka never once mentioned the Rovno Jews or Sosenki. For now, Isaac was a gentile from Russia. And religion and extermination were not discussed. They were forbidden subjects, approached only by the malicious. Even the disposition of the war was avoided. It didn't matter to them were the borders were. They belonged to no territory, fought for no country.

Isaac listened to Pietka chatter away about memories of Rovno, but at the same time he tried to piece together the last few hours, this sudden initiation into the community of men after eight months alone. When he tried to talk, he found himself stammering, tripping over his words. It had been a long time since he spoke his last complete sentence to another human being.

"It's a good name, Sergei, no?" Pietka asked.

"Who?"

"Sergioski, you!"

Isaac realized it was his new name. It kept his past and his family hidden from judgment. Pietka had chosen carefully. It meant, in Russian, a loving man, a man of heart, warm and easy to trust.

"Of course," Isaac exclaimed. "I'm Sergei from Kiev."

"Good. Good. Funny. I forgot your real name. I remembered your face but your name, I forgot it. What is it?"

"I'm Sergei from Kiev," Isaac responded so finally and so firmly that Pietka didn't bother to question. He just smiled. There were no more questions.

They moved into the woods with Isaac dragging the Mannlicher rifle with Mauser bolt action behind him in the dirt like it was a toy. It kicked up dust, plowing a trail behind Isaac. He felt comforted, nevertheless by the tug of the rifle. He was, in a sense, armed now. Once he got his strength back, he might even fight. So Isaac was left in the trail made by the rifle and Sergei, the newest member of the group, entered the Polish woods.

CHAPTER FIVE
THE JARS OF SAMOGON

For the first few weeks in this new society of war fugitives and exiles, Isaac tried desperately to contribute. But he did not seem to be gaining weight or strength. As the band of men moved about night after night, Isaac was relegated to the campsite, tending the fire, cleaning up, guarding the clearing while the rest were out searching for food, clothing, or recruits.

During the first nights, Isaac stayed close to the fire, his heart leaping at the sight of the warming flames. It had been his first hearth in countless months and it reminded him of fireplaces and simmering soups and hot tea. Exhausted as we was, he volunteered to stay by the fire all night, banking it, stoking it so that it would never go out. This would become his first duty for the men.

Through the subsequent weeks, Isaac stoked the fire and cooked the meals, whether it was chicken or watery stews or wild rabbit. But no matter how well he cooked, he had no appetite himself and ate little of what he prepared. He just could not thrive. He knew, in fact, he was getting thinner and even more sickly. But he hid his own debilitation behind the posture of a pleasant, cooperative boy, volunteering for everything and always assigned to stay behind. In fact, he was doing "business" as best he could, just as his father urged.

In those first weeks, Isaac observed the men and began to learn the rules of their "order." Clearly, Stepan was the self-appointed, unopposed leader. He was the strongest, the most dangerous, and the loudest. Pietka accepted the role of counsel and strategist, performing quietly and unobtrusively so that Stepan got all the credit for the operations carried out. For the most part, Stepan led them into brief raids on farmhouses, granaries, and, on occasion, market squares, where they demanded food and volunteers. More often than not, the villagers would comply with some foodstuffs and clothing. But sometimes, they would call the local police or try to alert the nearby military commandant. Then Stepan and his group would return empty-handed, even bruised or wounded.

On those occasions, Isaac proved his worth, quickly cleaning cuts or bullet wounds with leaves and special concoctions his brother had taught him made of flowers and roots. If he was lucky, there would even be sulfur packets or some alum to fight infection or check the bleeding. But medical supplies came only when they stumbled on a dead soldier and they could retrieve his medical kit. Isaac's patients quickly healed and returned to their duties. Stepan noticed this but still refused to acknowledge Isaac's existence.

Then one night, Isaac saw how brutal Stepan's rules could be. They had chosen a small clearing in the middle of a forest of sycamore and pine. A few of the newer recruits had set out on their own to ransack a poorly guarded military depot. Through sheer luck and good fortune, they attacked the depot a day after it had been abandoned. Exhilarated by their first military success, they took what little had been left behind and burned the rest. The raid had not been sanctioned by Stepan or even suggested by Pietka, so when the new comrades returned with their booty and prizes, Stepan was infuriated. To make matters worse, one of the new recruits, Aloysha, an engineer from the Polish army, had found a pair of Wehrmacht officer's boots. They had been polished to a high sheen and glowed with reflective light.

Aloysha strutted about, goose-stepping, joking about Bolsheviks and Jews. He was a blunt, vulgar, and brash young man, who obviously admired the Nazis and the efficiency of the SS from a distance. He was proud of his prize and swaggered and marched about proudly. The boots gleamed like an obsidian mirror. Compared to the suave cut and stylish lines of the boots, Aloysha appeared an incongruent, comical opposite. He wore a skimpy farmer's cap with limp ear flaps, a plain cloth windbreaker and a drab cotton sweater. The boots were clearly Aloysha's first extravagance in his young life, a momentary indulgence in vanity and decadence.

Even Isaac smiled at Aloysha's brashness, accepting the young man's politics as a symptom of youthful fervor. He did not sense a true and total hostility in Aloysha's manner. But Aloysha had broken a cardinal rule of the group. Never, never call attention to your personal possessions. In the midst of war, material worth far outweighed life itself. The more you collected and hid, the longer you might live when captured. A mood of moral and brutal greed pervaded this group.

That night, with Aloysha sleeping off in the distance like a baby, Stepan began to prowl. Isaac watched him from his place near the fire. The strong man would storm out to the edge of the clearing, vanish for a second in flickering darkness of the woods, then reappear about the circumference of the camp. He was circling nervously. Meanwhile Aloysha slept, his prized boots jutting out from under the army blanket like ebony trophies. Isaac pretended to fuss over the crackling fire: gathering more wood, poking at the center, sending sparks flying int the air. But all the time, he watched Stepan.

After about an hour Stepan stopped near Aloysha and spread out his bedroll right next to the young man's patent-leather Nazi boots. Aloysha did not stir. He was deep in sleep, dreaming, Isaac conjectured, about marching in a braided and decorated uniform with his goose-stepping boots gleaming in the air and young girls applauding wildly from windows and roofs. Stepan watched Aloysha carefully, kneeling by his bedding to arrange it, then checking Aloysha, then back to his blanket. Finally, certain that Aloysha was dead asleep, Stepan made his move. He lurched for Aloysha's boots, wrenching them off Aloysha's feet and dragging the young man with him for a distance as he pulled and tugged. Aloysha screamed, twisted his body, trying to wrest free from Stepan's tenacious grip on both his legs. Then, with both boots free and Stepan waving them victoriously in the air, Aloysha lost his head. He grabbed for his rifle, whipping it about so quickly that he had it pointed at Stepan even before he could release the safety. But Stepan had seen the move and was ready, dropping the boots and tearing his Mauser-38 pistol from inside his vest, cocking and firing in one motion. The bullet struck Aloysha square in the chest, sending his rifle flying in the air. Stepan fired once more at Aloysha's face, the bullet's impact knocking off the young man's rustic wool cap as it struck the bridge of his nose, ripping away all trace of his brash, blunt look. Isaac shuddered at the pistol shot and cringed at the sound of shattering bone. He could not look. It was over as quick at that. By the time the men had jumped to their feet, armed and ready, Stepan was giving the order to bury Aloysha, and indicating that it would be necessary to move again. Moments later Stepan appeared from the darkness of the woods, wearing Aloysha's boots proudly.

It was a lesson Isaac would not forget: Sleep with everything you own and hide what you treasure from view. Never take your boots off or even let them show from beneath your blanket. Better yet, instead of protecting your valuables, keep nothing valuable but the linen on your back.

A day after the incident, Stepan had insisted on setting up a new base and by the following night, Aloysha was forgotten.

As always, the men would leave early in the morning from the camp and Isaac would remain behind to guard the scattered belongings and remnants of displacement. It had grown almost impossible for Isaac to carry firewood or even carry a rucksack. His body had melted away, leaving nothing but a frame of tinder-thin bones and crepe-like muscles. That particular morning, Pietka noticed Isaac's difficulty with some wood and helped him lug a few larger pieces over to the fire. When he saw Stepan glaring at him, ready to declare Isaac a burden and misfit, Pietka made elaborate gestures to convey the heaviness of the wood.

"God, Sergei, this stuff must be made of stone. No wonder you're having problems." When Stepan turned away, he grabbed Isaac's arm and tenderly reassured him, "It's all right. Just try to get your strength back. Damn it, you always got the right medicine for the rest of us. Can't you whip up something for yourself?"

Isaac shook his head and shrugged. Pietka left, certain that Isaac would be dead in a few days if he could not reverse the alarming loss of weight. When the camp was empty, Isaac went to the larder, a large canvas bag hanging from a tree limb above ground and grabbed some bread and potatoes. He tried to stuff his mouth with the starch, even if his teeth and gums flared with pain with each bite he took. But he started to gag and lost all appetite. It seemed like his body had shrunk inside and out. There was no stomach left, no room for anything but a crust here, a sliver there. He couldn't even gorge himself if he wanted to.

He sat by the tree under the canvas larder and fell asleep, holding a heel of bread in one hand and a half-chewed potato in the other. But his hazy, shallow sleep was interrupted by a thud, then a crash of metal. Jerking into consciousness, he opened his eyes to the sight of a rifle pinpointed on him. When he tried to stand and protest, a hand pushed his shoulder down, then another rifle butt pressed against his left temple. He was surrounded by armed men.

When he had tome to look around, he saw more men, armed just like Stepan, with cartridge belts strapped across shoulder and waist. A short, stocky man with a gray, wiry beard grinned down at Isaac. The man's upper teeth jutted out at all angles over his lower lip. He wore a worn and dirt-patched sheepskin vest.

"Where are your friends?" he sneered at Isaac, jabbing him once with a sharp kick of his heel into his side.

Isaac felt the pain of that kick in his ribs while the buck-toothed man sneered at him. "Where are your friends?" He kicked again. "Well, are you telling us?!" Isaac felt the imprint of the man's boot in his side throb and burn. He could barely catch his breath. "I don . . . don't know."

A rifle bolt clicked into place. The stocky one with protruding teeth pushed a Luger into Isaac's ear. "What are you—Pole, Bolshy? Doesn't matter. You're dead."

From the corner of his eye, Isaac saw a tall figure in an improvised stretcher made of blankets and long branches. He was tossing about feverishly. Even though sick or wounded, he was obviously too important to leave behind.

"It doesn't matter." Isaac spoke in a strained voice. His heart was racing in his chest like it was about to explode. "If you take anything from the camp, my friends will kill me anyway. Either way, it doesn't matter."

The figure in the stretcher screamed and the stocky man turned to his comrade angrily, clearly disturbed by the man's pain. Seeing the writhing figure in such anguish, he snarled back at Isaac with vengeance, "Maybe we'll shoot you in the hip, like they did my friend over there. And let you suffer."

The rest of the men stood, waiting for an order. They were

smeared with mud, their jackets and shirts torn and grimy. Isaac could tell by their appearance that these were bandits, as Pietka had called them. Worse than any marauding group in the forest, they robbed and killed, willing to work for any side if the rewards were right. But mostly, they'd terrorize villagers and farmers. There were even rumors of abduction and rape. Isaac had been warned by Pietka, these bandits were a mean and desperate sort, an angry collection of misfits and criminals.

Then Isaac noticed the wounded man trying to sit up. His size and strength were obvious, as he pushed away one of his comrades trying to restrain him. With one swipe of the arm, he knocked his compatriot backwards off his feet. But as soon as he tried to stand up, his legs buckled and his sudden burst of energy drained quickly. He collapsed head-first off the stretcher, crashing down into the scrub brush. Many men ran over to assist him and make him comfortable. It was clear he had been held in high esteem.

"Let's get what we want from here and get out...now!" the stocky man insisted, his wiry beard bristling. He shifted his weight nervously, then shouted out an order in a voice twitching with fury. He snapped his fingers and a thin man, wearing an oversized Polish army overcoat, stepped up to guard Isaac. He shoved the muzzle of his carbine into Isaac's chest, then snapped the bolt back.

"Wait...," Isaac pleaded. He grabbed the arm of his guard, startling him by his touch. "Tell them, I can help with that sick man over there. Tell your comrades, I can help him. I know medicine. He needs medical help." Isaac rambled on quickly, afraid to stop and give the guard a chance to reject his propositions. "I do it all the time with my group—fix bones, clean wounds, remove bullets..."

His tirade of services worked. The guard shouted towards

the edge of the camp, where the wounded man lay. The man with the protruding teeth was kneeling by the stretcher when he heard the guard call. After hearing what Isaac had said, he mulled over for a second all the possibilities. The guard, still holding Isaac close by the barrel of his carbine, asked him, "Is he worse?"

"Yes."

"What do we have to lose?"

There was desperation and no small bit of resignation in the final decision. The guard was ordered to direct Isaac toward the wounded. The stocky man followed, stood by when they reached the stretcher, and shouted out Isaac's options in frustration. "Fix him. Make him comfortable. If you save him, maybe we'll spare you. You better do your Goddamned best."

Isaac looked down at the wounded man. He was shaking, ashen-faced, his breath shallow, his eyes half-rolled back, and his hands clenching and opening in spasms of pain. Throwing back the covers, Isaac saw the bullet wound. It was in the upper thigh. He carefully separated the cloth of his breeches from the entry wall of the bullet, now dry and caked with blood. Then he probed the oozing wound with his finger wrapped in cloth, feeling for the bullet. He discovered, luckily, that the bullet had lodged superficially near the bone, missing the femoral artery. If Isaac stayed alert, and managed not to collapse, he might be able to remove the metal and clean the wound.

"For pain?" he asked a man standing at the head of the stretcher. "Do you have anything? Medical kits... anything?" The man considered the request, then whistled to his confederates stationed as sentries in the woods. There were shouts, then one of the sentries suddenly appeared carrying a large canvas bag full of jars. Isaac could hear the sloshing of the liquid and rattling of the glass inside the bag. Pulling out a round canning jar, the sentry twisted off the top and offered the contents to his friends first. The sharp smell of alcohol was unmistakable. The leader with the wiry beard and splayed teeth took a sip, shivered, then smiled crookedly. Another bandit offered the jar to the wounded man, but the injured man could barely recognize faces, much less respond. So the liquor was forced down his throat. Someone else offered another jar to Isaac who shook it off. The bandit was shocked.

"It's Samogon, the best. Our women make it at home. In our kettles. With our fires. It's not good enough for you?"

"No," Isaac nervously responded, "I'm sure it's the finest . . . I just need to concentrate."

There was a groan and then some laughter at Isaac's refusal. Most of the men assumed he was just too young and inexperienced to take a sip of this potent home brew. But no one interfered or forced Isaac. He was allowed to continue.

So Isaac began. He first cleaned the wound with some of the Samogon, used a piece of gauze from a recovered medical kit to wrap his finger, then gently poked once more into the wound until he caught the lip of the bullet. With more careful and delicate movement, he managed to draw the bullet out. All the while, the patient, constantly fed the Samogon, groaned and winced in a feverish stupor. Isaac then applied a poultice of sulphur, also recovered from packets found in medical kits, mixed in with a decoction of leaves, flowers, and roots. He had prepared such an infusion of natural ingredients days before for his own men.

Nearing the end, he packed the wound with a layer of wet leaves, wrapped the thigh with cloth torn from a drying shirt found in camp and tied it carefully with a loose strip of linen. Finally, he forced the contents of one additional packet of sulphur dissolved in the Samogon down the injured man's throat. Finishing the last procedure, he was done.

Exhausted, dizzy with weakness, and worn by the tightening pain in his gut, Isaac sat down on the ground and waited. In a few minutes, the patient grew quieter. He stopped tossing about and mumbling in pain. For the first time since entering camp, the wounded man was on the verge of a deep, restful sleep. The bandits were astounded. But the stocky one with the prominent and vicious row of teeth was suspicious. He always saw malevolence in any outsider's behavior. Grabbing Isaac's thick hair, he pulled the boy's head back.

"You're just a boy, a piece of green crap, a shit! How do you know all this?"

Isaac coughed and tried to whisper an answer with his head and neck bent back by the taut grip.

"Family," he answered hoarsely.

"I don't know if you helped or not. Maybe not. Maybe he's just dying. Who knows?"

"Please," Isaac reminded him. "Please leave the camp alone. You steal or destroy anything and I am dead. They'll blame it all on me. Please."

"I see," he loosened his grip on Isaac's hair as he suddenly had a thought. Then he broke out again in that snarling, rodent-like smile he had, hiding a nasty snarl behind every grin and jutting tooth.

"I'll give you a chance. Only one." He whispered to the man in the oversize coat, then consulted with another bandit. Finally, he was ready. "You want to be a man, right? Of course. Look at you, though. There's not much hope. But I'll give you a chance."

He snapped his fingers and someone brought him a jar of Samogon. "If you can drink this full jar of Samogon down to the bottom without puking on us and messing up, I'll call you a soldier and a real man and leave you and the camp alone. Well?"

"I don't understand," Isaac was unprepared for this, "Please, I don't understand the conditions..."

"Drink this jar of Samogon down without puking and we'll spare you and the camp. If you get sick like some nauseous kid, we'll just have to put you out of your misery. A promise! One shot and you're out of your misery."

Isaac looked up at the twisted face. He was sure they were making some kind of joke once again at his expense. Just before they killed him.

"Is that a deal, boy? Hold our Samogon down and we will leave. Puke like a bawling baby and it's all over. For good. Fair?"

Isaac nodded, remembering with a shudder those awful moments when his parents would let him sip some schnapps or drink down some thick, syrupy ceremonial wine. It was always a strong drink, but nothing could prepare him for the taste of Samogon. Even from a distance, the fumes from an opened jar of brew hit Isaac's mouth and nose. It smelled like the medicine cabinet in his brother's clinic.

"I'll drink it." He looked toward the sky, bright and peaceful above him. Such a glorious day and all these men can do is torture another human being. On such days in the past, Isaac could never think of injustices or ghastly acts and misdeeds. But he could think only of horror today, even with the summer weather. It seemed to Isaac, in fact, that the only weather suitable for the world he lived in was a deluge, the deluge. Wash all of them away in one great universal inundation. Cleanse the globe, scrub the grubs and slugs and snakes of mankind off the surface of the earth. Then start with a fresh batch, a new crop of mankind. A race of innocent and compassionate souls. Not this! Not these bandits or the rest of the barbarians. This was a race of criminals.

"Let me have the jar. I'll drink it."

There was laughter and some clapping; this was clearly entertainment for these men.

The grimy jar was handed to Isaac. He sloshed the clear liquid around, sat back against a tree trunk to brace himself and began to drink.

As the liquid burned its way down, setting fire to nose and throat, gullet and belly, Isaac kept praying for that deluge, a great torrent of rain and gust of wet wind that would wash it all away: bandits, forests, armies, and the caustic, searing flames of Samogon pouring down inside him. But there was no downpour. The sun grew even hotter; a few wispy clouds sailed by and Isaac kept drinking from the jar.

His insides turned over. It was as if his intestines and stomach were splitting open. He even felt his toes heat up, his legs throb with darts of flame. He couldn't keep his eyes open, but when he closed them, all he saw were swirls of stars and exploding meteors. He kept drinking.

The men began to stomp and clap in rhythm, urging him on, enjoying the spectacle. Finally, he drained the last drop and held the empty jar aloft. But he was spinning with confusion and the jar dropped from his grasp, shattering on the rock. Isaac then looked up at the wiry beard and crooked teeth, and defiantly proclaimed, "I am done." Some of the men cheered, but then they quieted down, waiting for Isaac to be sick. He remained against the tree trunk, almost motionless, apparently placid, and so stupefied he was comfortable. Inside, he felt his whole body lurching and wrenching this way and that, but he refused to give these bandits their execution. What little will he had left, he exercised. He managed to keep the nausea swirling up inside him from overtaking his body. He coughed, he burped, then stood up, shakily, to announce, "It's over. You must leave!" A number of the bandits smiled, secretly enjoying Isaac's triumph. But the stocky leader was dumbfounded. He was sure this was some sort of trick. He examined the jar, he examined Isaac's clothing for hidden tubes; he even examined the tree trunk. But he did not renege. There was some shred of honor left in the tattered world.

One by one, the bandits retreated into the woods, leaving the camp intact. When the stretcher was carried out, the stocky leader followed, his jaw set, his upper row of teeth biting down in frustration on his lower lip. And just as suddenly as they came, they were gone. The camp was, for the most part, untouched. Isaac had successfully defended it like a soldier.

But now with the pressure off, with the criminals gone, he could submit to the real waves of sickness over taking him. He had prayed to the almighty that this feeling might go away altogether, but only half his wish was granted. He was violently nauseous only after the bandits left.

He tried to rush towards the nearby stream, hoping to plunge into the water, drenching his head, flooding his insides with cool spring water. But as soon as he got to the top of the small hill overlooking the river, he was stricken. The Samogon opened him up like a sluicing floodgate. He began to vomit, convulsively, in constant waves and spasms. He could do nothing else. His body was wracked and twisted as he continued to spew, the violence of the retching throwing him to the ground.

He rolled down the hill, vomiting and coughing. Then he tried to stand and was hit once more by a violent wave, and slammed to the ground again in a convulsive spasm, rolling and heaving. Isaac felt as if all that he had eaten these past eight months streamed out of his belly. All the grass and cabbages and bark and roots, all the forest nuts and berries, all the mushrooms poured out in a dark amber stream. It was as if his body had never really digested any of it.

He climbed back towards the river, felt engulfed by another wave of nausea, withstood it, then heaved forward by a new spasm. But he kept on until he could drop to his knees and immerse his pounding head into the stream.

For over an hour, Isaac was sick. By the end he was squeezed dry until his whole body was bruised and tender, inside and out. But after an hour, he was still alive. He had grown even more thirsty, drinking handfuls of water one after another. He had never felt this thirsty before. After minutes of kneeling at the stream and drinking incessantly with cupped hands by the banks, Isaac felt calmer. He curled up and went to sleep.

It was Pietka who awakened him by evening. "You look awful. What happened?"

"I defended the camp against bandits. I kept it safe."

"Are you all right?"

Isaac stood up once more. He felt lighter, but more relaxed inside, as if all his vital organs, his whole digestive system was split wide open. And he was hungry for the first time in months. Naturally hungry for good food. He had not been truly hungry for eight months and, in spite of the offerings, he had not been truly hungry since he entered the forest. But now his mouth watered. He could imagine and taste delicacies. It was as if his insides had been closed and shriveled, but now the Samogon had opened it all up, cleansing him. He was so hungry, he could eat a thousand dinners.

Making him sit, Pietka brought over a large chunk of bread and cheese to eat, which Isaac quickly devoured. Then jumping to his feet with renewed sense of purpose, Isaac exclaimed to his friend, "You know, Pietka, if you don't mind, I'd love to eat some more."

He was insatiably hungry and would remain so for days. "Some more bread, Sergei?"

"Yes . . . and . . . "

"What . . . some potatoes?"

"Yes . . . and some vegetables. Everything. More of everything!!"

That night, Isaac slept feeling full and satisfied. The next morning, he was hungry again and feasted on larger portions than anyone in the camp.

By the end of the week, he could feel his strength returning. Instead of schlepping his rifle about by a strap or a string, he could now lift it and hold it gamely to his shoulders. It was not a toy anymore that he dragged along. It was a weapon.

A week later, he insisted on going with his friends on their next foray into town or countryside for food. He convinced the men that his mastery of the languages would make him an invaluable asset. Stepan protested at first, convinced Isaac's life was superfluous from the start. But he had to relent under pressure. He agreed to supply Isaac with a few clips, enough rounds to defend himself. He was also issued new hiking shoes and a dagger. Isaac put the knife in his belt and lifted his rifle to his shoulder.

Armed and ready, Isaac listened for the signal: a whistle. Pietka checked him over, tightening the cartridge belt slung across his narrow frame. Then he waited for Stepan to lead them. The whistle was suddenly sounded, long and harmonic. Isaac embraced Pietka affectionately as a comrade-in-arms and then set out with the rest to march into the woods.

He left the fire and the cooking behind, the frailty and innocence, Rovno and Volhynia; and he advanced with the rest into action. And like the rest, Isaac was now a soldier.

CHAPTER SIX
KOLPAK'S BRIGADE

Everything had gone wrong for Stepan's "warriors." In spite of Stepan's reassurance that the farmhouse near Kobryn belonged to his distant cousin, Isaac and his comrades did not find warmth and hospitality. First, Novak and Stepan tried the back door, but it was locked and barred. Stepan ordered Isaac to try the front entrance. That, too, was shuttered closed. Stepan then banged heavily on the door, but no one answered. Finally, running out of what little patience he had, Stepan took out his Schmeiser MP-38, a machine-gun pistol, and smashed at the door with the stock. Still no one responded.

Pietka and Isaac drew back, waiting uneasily in the yard by the twisted frame of a collapsed, worm-eaten farm wagon abandoned in the backyard of the house. Even from their distant post, they could recognize the sighs of Stepan's growing fury.

Normally, these operations for food and clothing seldom resulted in any violence or gunfire, and never in serious casualties. All efforts were made to maintain the trust and friendship of the villagers or merchants so that Stepan's men could return again and again for more supplies. In fact, it was only Stepan in all of the foraging operations who threatened the villagers or the farmers; it was only Stepan who ever brandished his weapon menacingly at some merchant or housewife. And it was only Stepan who looked forward to engaging the Nazi Einsatzkommando units or the local police in battle. Stepan never changed. He felt invincible and remained headstrong, intimidating, and brutal.

Still, no one dared challenge him as he led Isaac and his comrades farther and farther east into White Russia, near Pinsk and its marshes, and nearer to the retreating German army. It was already the early Spring of 1943, many months after the Nazi defeat at Stalingrad, and Stepan was leading his troops blindly into the retreating Nazis as they were chased by the Russians from Kharkov, Rostov, and then from Kiev. As the bitter winter ended and the Russian offensive consolidated, Stepan grew even fiercer.

Now he was on the doorstep of a friendly relative, a female cousin on his mother's side. He expected cooperation and generosity. Not this! Not a barricaded house, not locks and bars against a relative. Stepan kicked at the door again and again while he smashed at it with his weapon. Finally, it began to splinter and the hinges split. He and Novak quickly entered. But there was still no one. However, signs of life were everywhere, with the large wooden table in the kitchen still set for breakfast with cups, bowls, and plates still splattered with food, along with bread and cheese strewn about half-eaten. A fire smoldered yet in the dark iron hulk of the stove. There was an apron over one chair, some horse tackle over another.

Stepan yelled out, "Elena! Stepan is here!" There was no answer. Novak relaxed, almost relieved there would be no confrontation. He quickly undraped the bags he carried over his shoulder and started filling them with bread and cheese.

"What are you doing?" Stepan growled. "I want my people to get us the supplies."

"But there's no one here, Stepan. They're gone. No one else is going to..."

Stepan erupted before Novak could finish. He kicked over the chairs one by one, and swept the crockery off the table with the butt of his machine gun.

Just at that moment, outside in the yard by the side of the house, the root-cellar door opened and three young children started creeping out of their hiding place, startled by the sound of Stepan's voice and the breaking dishes inside. Isaac and Pietka watched their escape with amusement and satisfaction, neither uttering a sound. First, the young boy of eight sped across the yard onto a nearby road; then he whistled and the two younger girls followed him. As the girls started across the yard noisily, Novak caught sight of them through the window. He screamed out, "Stop!" and Stepan whirled about, his Schmeiser pointed through the open door, firing indiscriminately. He sprayed the yard with bullets, forcing Pietka and Isaac to leap for cover behind the wagon. But the girls were already out of range. At the sound of the machine gun, screams could be heard from inside the house. "You want us. Only us!" Elena, her husband, and her mother-in-law rushed into the kitchen from wherever they were hiding inside the house, hands raised. Elena screamed again, "You want us! We will help! Take us! Leave the children alone!"

Hearing the pleas and shouts behind him, Stepan abruptly stopped shooting at the escaping children and wheeled around to face his cousin. There was fury in his eyes as he glared at Elena, adjusting the gun on his hip so it pointed directly at her. Then, in an angry, almost violent outburst, he demanded food, clothing, and supplies for his men. When the husband protested, trying to explain how scarce everything was, Stepan ordered him to sit at the table, jamming the snub-nosed barrel of the machine gun into his chest.

Soon Elena and her mother-in-law were rushing about filling the supply bags. At one point, Stepan yelled out an order to Isaac in the yard to make sure his cousin slaughtered some chickens for the men. Isaac approached Elena shyly, embarrassed by the rough commands of his leader, and held out the bag. She stared at him, then at the proffered bag, then looked towards the kitchen where Stepan stood guard and spat contemptuously in his direction. Isaac was amazed but did nothing except open the bag wider. Without a moment's hesitation, Elena spun around, snared a cackling chicken by its neck, stretched the neck across a thick fence post, grabbed the ax leaning against this blood spattered post, and with one incredibly smooth blow, chopped the head off. She repeated the process twice, then stood facing Isaac, holding the carcasses of the bleeding chickens in one hand and the bloody ax in the other. Abruptly, she flung the chickens inside the bag.

Stepan was smiling as much as he ever could at all the activity about him. He had insisted to his men that this house would bring a bounty. After all, this was "family."

With Stepan's machine gun still trained on the husband, the women rushed about until there were three large cloth bags full of supplies. At that point, Stepan laughed with satisfaction even while he continued to threaten the puffy-eyed husband with his gun.

Then it happened. The fleeing children must have flagged down a convoy of local authorities and German officers, for suddenly two military vehicles came roaring into the back yard off the dirt road, screeching and skidding to a stop. One vehicle carried four local policemen, the other three Nazi officers. Pietka, standing guard on the perimeter of the farm, saw them coming and discharged a few rounds into the air as warning shots. Then he was cut off from access to the house as the vehicles swerved in front of him and drove up to the kitchen door itself. Pietka fired a few more rounds directly at the vehicle as he shouted to alert the men. When the Nazi officers spotted Pietka, they started firing back, forcing him to retreat across the field towards the woods.

Isaac heard Pietka's warning and watched through the window as Pietka charged away from the fire towards the forest. His heart sank as he saw some of the police fire directly at his friend. Pietka stumbled once, fell into the furrows and lay still for a moment. At that sight, Isaac felt a fleeting sense of isolation, a stabbing ache reminding him that Pietka was his only link to Rovno, to his childhood, to his real identity. It was only with Pietka he could share bits and pieces of personal history. Only Pietka could make him laugh, and now his friend was lying in the cabbage field, cut down by German bullets. Isaac felt totally adrift again among strangers without any feelings, without any sense of belonging. Then, almost as if he was urged on by Isaac's longings, Pietka jumped to his feet, scrambled on for a moment, flung himself to the ground again, then quickly rose and ran again. It was Pietka's plan to fall and rise, stumble and then run, creating confusion and a poor target for the gunmen. Somehow it worked and Pietka stumbled across the field into the woods and safety.

It was all happening in an instant. As soon as Pietka was safe, Isaac turned with Novak to escape through the front door. But the husband tried to stop them. He had escaped from his guarded position at the kitchen table when Stepan turned his sights on arriving vehicles. Now the husband tried to block Novak and Isaac from leaving. Before Isaac could push this sad-eyed man out of his way, Stepan had glanced back, saw the husband escaping and opened fire. The husband, struck by Stepan's bullets, bounced backwards out of Isaac's reach, smashed against the front and fell forward stiff and solid as a statue.

When Novak tried to pull Stepan out of the house, he was pounded away by a fist. "What is this? Running away?" Stepan railed at him. "What for! No one's going to kill me. No one! Not ever! Stay and fight! You'll be safe with me. Stay and fight!" Even as he yelled, he turned his MP-38 towards the door, emptying all the rounds into the vehicle containing the local police. Before the men had time to disembark, they were dead. Novak bolted at the sound of the machine gun and ran with Isaac through the front door, leaving only Stepan to fight.

Dropping his empty Schmeiser to the floor, Stepan now pulled out a Luger from a side holster and unstrapped his Mauser rifle from his shoulder. Armed with both weapons, he began to systematically kill each Nazi officer as they rushed through the kitchen door. It was too easy. Neither the local police nor the Nazis had any idea who was firing at them. They planned to simply enter, subdue, and arrest the thieves. They could never have imagined the one-man arsenal that stood in their way. Standing full abreast of them, at the door, not even hiding behind a stick of furniture, Stepan fired away with the Luger in one hand, the Mauser rifle under his other arm, his giant figure and broad shoulders barely shaking from the recoil of the weapons.

By this time, Novak and Isaac were running in panic towards the cover of the nearby woods. They heard Stepan shout in triumphant glee as he finished off the last soldier. Then he spotted the mother-in-law cowering near the pantry. She looked up at Stepan with bewildered, almost astonished eyes, crouching beneath the wooden counter, its surface heavily scarred by knife ridges and cleaver marks. Stepan studied her face for a moment, saw she was about to scream, and quickly reloaded. With the loud click and metallic snap of the bolt, she threw her arms around her head protectively as if to ward off any bullets with her arms. With that, Stepan shot her through the top of her head with one bullet.

Then gathering up the bags full of supplies, he started out, exhilarated and buoyant. There he stood at the kitchen door, amidst the carnage, victorious and unhurt. As he started quickly towards the fields, his arms wrapped around the heavy bags, he could only think of the adulation and glory awaiting him from his men, so he never saw his cousin Elena at the corner of the house watching him. He never looked back once to see her tug a Browning rifle from the grip of a dead Nazi, and he barely heard the click of the bolt as she aimed at him, shaking and hysterical with grief. Even though she was no more than ten feet from him, the first shot was wild, striking his shoulder. He stumbled forward dropping the bags, the searing pain in his shoulder paralyzing his arm for a moment. Then whirling about, he reached with his arm for his Luger, but Elena had already squeezed the trigger and held it down. She braced herself against the side of the house as she did, emptying round after round into Stepan. Her finger froze on the trigger while her body jerked back and forth with each kick of the discharge. But she did not waver or relax. Stepan was driven back by the impact, speechless and startled. He threw out his arms to fend off the bullets, then stumbled forward and collapsed. Elena kept clicking the trigger long after the chamber was empty, her arms trembling with the vibration of the rifle and the passion of her vengeance.

She held the rifle at dead aim on her cousin, squeezing the trigger over and over even though there were no bullets left. Stepan lifted his head once, trying to say her name, but only bloody froth filled his throat. He coughed, shuddered and died. It was only then that Elena dropped the rifle and turned away.

That night, Isaac waited for Pietka to return while the rest of the men shuffled about warily, expecting Stepan to reappear at any minute. There was little conversation. Isaac remained by the fire, stoking it, banking the earth, startled by every noise in the woods. He, too, expected Stepan to come charging out of the high grass and spiky brush with bags full of food, bragging about his victims and extolling his murderous soul. He fully expected Stepan to then turn on the cowards who deserted

him and kill them all in one spray of bullets. But no one returned that evening, neither Stepan nor Pietka.

By midnight, the camp had gone to sleep. Isaac and Wasic
had volunteered to stay up and stand guard. There was a scarci-
ty of food and there would have to be new operations planned,
new forays into the countryside without Stepan or Pietka. Isaac
understood this, and also knew that either Wasic or Novak
would attempt to assume the mantle of Stepan in a matter of
days. He would have to readjust, prepare to go on once again
with new rules, new orders, and new leaders.

Near morning, Isaac awoke to the sound of a low-flying
plane. Everyone quickly scurried for cover, dragging their
bedrolls and possessions with them into the heavy brush. The
plane seemed to circle for an hour, then pass. Warily the men
returned to the clearing, unsure of their next move. Without
their demagogue, Stepan, and their strategist, Pietka, they had
little direction. Wasic tried to step in. He was Polish, a farmer from Lublin, with a barrel chest, stocky build, and bowlegs.
He wore the drab brown tunic of a Polish soldier. His bellig-
erent presence and compact power made him Stepan's natural successor. By mid-morning, he was trying to read the few
maps Stepan left behind. In spite of Isaac's obvious intelligence
and facility with language, Wasic was not about to involve this
young man in any activities. Wasic had never been convinced
of Isaac's Russian origins. He was suspicious of Pietka's scheme
to give Isaac a new identity, but he could not pinpoint any flaws
or refutable facts. Isaac simply remained an enigma to men like
Wasic, a hostile and threatening enigma.

While Wasic looked over the maps with some of his other
friends, a shout came out of the woods. Everyone jumped to
their feet, grabbed and cocked their weapons, aiming in the
general direction of the sound. But Isaac recognized the voice
immediately. "Don't shoot, you idiots! It's me, Pietka! I hope

you haven't forgotten me already. Pietka! The one with the giggle and laugh." Then Pietka broke out in laughter almost to prove his point. It was a nervous, but genuinely mocking chuckle directed as much towards himself as to others. He then stepped through the screen of trees and bushes into the clearing, carrying a large bag. Behind him stood another man, his hands raised in the air, palms open. This man wore a Russian army tunic and a flat wool Russian cap.

"Look men, the jackpot!" Pietka emptied the bag onto the ground, spilling out loaves of bread, potatoes, cans of American and Russian army rations.

Wasic, unconvinced and suspicious, still held his Browning rifle on Pietka.

Pietka looked at him, checked faces for Stepan and realized who was taking charge. "Wasic, you onion brain, this is what we've been waiting for. Where's Stepan?"

There was a murmur, but no definite reply. "Well," Pietka capitalized upon the uncertainty, "Stepan would have agreed. This is what he was waiting for. No more begging or sneaking about. We're going to be soldiers, not thieves."

Wasic still kept his rifle aimed at the stranger and asked, "Who is this one?"

"Mikhail. A Russian adviser. He's a friend, Wasic. Sent to help coordinate all the groups in these woods. To help us prepare... For God's sake, put the gun down. He's the one who brought all this food. He can bring us weapons and supplies."

Wasic reluctantly lowered his weapon and Pietka beamed. He put his arm around Mikhail and brought him over to Wasic, making them both shake hands. Then he went about the camp joking, slapping his comrades on the back, only stopping at Isaac. He grinned with relief, his eyes suddenly sad and sympathetic, and hugged his old friend. Once more, Isaac thought with relief, the uneasy balance between his past and the present had been restored. With Pietka back, situations would be bearable and the future possible, if not desirable.

Pietka quickly remembered his other purpose, rushed back to the bag and pulled out a handful of flyers, clutching them high in the air. "Read these, men. We have a meeting to go to in a few days. Mikhail will lead us there." He then tossed the flyers into the air and the men grabbed them. Even Wasic couldn't resist. It was a Russian army flyer, with information printed in Polish, German, and Ukrainian, announcing an organization meeting to be conducted by Commander Kolpak, head of the partisan resistance.

While the other men mulled over the flyer and distributed the new supplies, Pietka brought Mikhail over to Isaac. "Mikhail, I want you to meet the runt of the litter." With a mischievous gleam in his eye and a nod, Pietka continued. "We call him Sergei. He says he's from the Urals or the Caucasus; I forget which hills."

Mikhail grabbed Isaac's hand with both of his and shook it vigorously, speaking a mixture of Georgian and Moldavian accents. Isaac replied carefully in a Russian accent molded by his academic study and the memory of his father's Russian speech acquired from numerous trips into the Steppes. Mikhail was impressed and kissed Isaac suddenly on both cheeks while Pietka stood back enjoying the masquerade with a gleeful smile.

When Mikhail started briefing the group on this new Russian organization and the meeting with the great and heroic Commander Kolpak, Pietka took Isaac aside, whispering to him while Isaac tried to follow the Russian. "Think of it, Sergei; finally we can do more than hide and sleep, steal and run. Soldiers! Think of it. Of course, you might be too skinny and short for these Bolsheviks. They're all at least eight feet tall. Cossacks, you know, every one of them. While you, poor Sergei, are just a bedbug from Rovno." He smiled slyly as Isaac jabbed him smartly in the side with his fist. Then, in a shift of tone, Pietka grabbed Isaac's arm, squeezing it warmly and excitedly. "Best of all, no more Stepan! Right? Even if he came back from wherever he is, even if he came back from the dead—if anyone can do it, Stepan can—he won't be pushing us around anymore." Isaac nodded in agreement and shuddered inside at the thought of Stepan's yellowish apparition suddenly appearing in the shafts of sunlight pouring through the trees. If anyone could come back from the dead, it would be Stepan.

For the next two days, Mikhail led the men through the woods towards the meeting place where the Russian commander, Kolpak, was to speak and miraculously transform the bandits, robbers and marauders prowling the Polessi woods into a cohesive and formidable military resistance. Wasic, trying to think like Stepan, rejected the notion that any foreign country could tell him or his men what to do, especially Russia. And he had convinced some of the others to reject any overtures by this Kolpak.

By the late afternoon of the third day, Mikhail brought them to a large, simply constructed house, where the meeting would take place. The house itself, with its crude white plaster sides and overhanging timbered roof, had been used in the past as a rest station for travelers, a command post for government forestry workers, and an occasional lodging for royalty or politicians on the hunt.

A crowd of many different soldiers, citizens, partisans and bandits had assembled along with Isaac's group. In fact, Isaac was unnerved by the sight of so many people. He had forgotten what a crowd felt like. It brought back that disturbing sense of collective momentum which could pull individuals inexorably towards whatever fatal precipice some outside authority picked. He fought against the urge and deliberately stayed apart from everyone as much as possible.

All around, there was a babble of accents from all countries and walks, each group talking quietly, hushed by their own sense of defenselessness. Guards and sentries had been set up by both the Russian advisors and representatives from the various bands of men. No one really trusted anyone else for security arrangements, so the site was ringed about with a solid circle of armed men, dressed in a variety of military combinations—Austrian mess jackets from the Great War worn with modern German breeches; patchwork overcoats from Lithuania covering sheepskin vests from Estonia; Polish military tunics crisscrossed with black ammunition belts stolen from dead Nazi officers; padded vests from the Polish police worn over baggy overalls from a Ukrainian farmhouse.

Everyone stopped talking when a small convoy of Russian trucks appeared. They came from the east. The rumor was that an American plane had transported Kolpak from Moscow to a clearing a few kilometers away from this house. With the Americans flying regular supply missions into Russia and bombing raids over Germany, this particular plane had special orders cut both by the western Allies and the Russian premier.

The crowd cleared a path for the trucks and waited. From the canvas-hooped backs of the trucks came armed Russian soldiers with rifles strapped to their shoulders. They stood at attention by the trucks as Commander Kolpak appeared. Isaac could barely make out the trucks at first since the crowd and the height of the men blocked his view. But when he climbed on top of a rubble of bricks near the house, he caught a clear view of this leader, Kolpak. Isaac was disappointed. The commander stood no more than five feet, ten inches with a stocky but unremarkable build. His windburned face was clean shaven and lined by leathery creases and rugged folds. He looked more like a mountain climber or sheep herder than a military hero. Isaac had heard he was a highly decorated major, a popular military hero, from the Caucasus, born in Tblisi, the capital of Georgia, and trained as a soldier in the Ukraine.

With all that, he looked exactly the opposite of what he was supposed to be. He wore no military uniform, displayed no medals or military decorations. Instead, he was dressed in a white Georgian peasant blouse with multicolored braiding down the center, a thick rope around his waist, and a pair of simple wool breeches, more common to the farmers of the steppes than to a soldier of Moscow. He wore no soldier's hat either. It was a lambswool cap with ear flaps tied up in the center.

From all the rumors about his reputation, Isaac expected someone with shoulders as broad as Prometheus and tall as Goliath. Instead, everything about this man seemed average and common. This was someone, Isaac recalled, who had been brought up in Tblisi by the slopes of Mount Kazbek in the Caucasus. That was the mountain in legend where Prometheus, the maker of men, had been bound but never defeated. It was near the mythical valleys where Jason sought the Golden Fleece and giants ruled the caves. A land invaded by Arabs, Mongols, Persians, and Turks, but never conquered. This was Kolpak's legacy.

As the commander walked toward the house, Isaac noticed his high, fur-lined boots and the small military pistol strapped to his side. Somehow the sight of the man, though disappointing, was also reassuring. This was no Stepan, no Godtz. He was neither tyrant nor despot, brute nor bully. For a brief moment, he looked directly at Isaac as he scanned the crowd. His eyes were luminous, his expression compassionate and gentle. He laughed and joked, just like Pietka, with some men near him, as he moved through the crowd. With that one look and the sound of his laughter, Isaac began to understand the magnetism of his Commander Kolpak.

When the commander got to the entrance of the house and saw that the crowds could not be accommodated inside, he demanded that a few of the men hoist him to the sloping timber roof. Then he climbed a bit up the steep pitch, propped one leg behind him for balance, and raised his arms. The crowd all looked up. Just before he started to speak, Isaac turned towards one of the trucks and noticed three women seated in the shadowy interior dressed in gray Russian nurses' outfits. They all seemed nervous and shy, leaning back against the canvas sides to avoid the glances of the men outside. But one face in particular attracted Isaac. She was thinner than the rest, more delicate in features, with great scoops of brown for eyes that looked out in a kind of wonder at the crowd. Then, like so many times before when Isaac spied on girls, she caught him looking, and she stared back disquietingly. As in the past, Isaac felt a sudden wave of shame and humiliation sweep over him. He was guilty of invading a woman's privacy. But this woman was not embarrassed. Somehow she leaned out of the shadows and her delicate face with the wondrous eyes acknowledged Isaac and smiled back, warmly. Isaac assumed she had recognized someone else and turned away awkwardly, back to the roof and Kolpak. But even as he watched and listened, the face of this woman hovered before him in the air. He could not shake the look of her eyes.

Then Kolpak's voice awakened Isaac from his romantic reverie. This man from the mountains spoke in a simple, touching manner. His voice radiated a certain humility and honesty. His rough Slavic accent mixed Polish with Ukrainian, but somehow he made himself understood by all, drawing each listener to his cause, enrapturing the crowd with his passion.

"We have gathered here for one purpose," Kolpak reminded them. "Every one of us wants to go home. Every one of us wants to go back to what we love and what we were forced to leave. We are all here to reclaim our place in our homeland, and to return our nation to its people." There were shouts of agreement and cheers from the crowd. "I will not ask you to bleed for me. You are not fighting for me. I will not ask you to lay down your life willingly for some military scheme worked out by fat and distant generals from countries you will never visit. No! There is only one cause worth suffering for. Each of you has such a cause inside you and it is yours alone. Each of you has already decided what you will suffer and die for. I am only here to help you in your cause. Join us for that. We can supply you with food, fuel, and ammunition; we can train you so that you will be equal to any soldier you fight. We can guide you and protect you. But only if you are convinced there is a prize worth all this danger and battle. I am confident we will fight together. I am convinced we can rally together into one brave and powerful army of partisans. And I promise you we will defeat the invaders and the traitors and the criminals, and we will all return home. Will you join! Will you share in that victory!"

The crowd cheered and clapped as he went on. Each time he talked of home, there was a reaction. Each time he mentioned "victory," there was a collective shout of approval. Even Isaac found himself applauding wildly half way through the speech, without once considering who he would return to, what home or country he would reclaim.

Nevertheless by the end of Kolpak's speech, the men rushed towards him. Everyone wanted to shake his hand and pledge their support. Some held back, like Wasic, but when he saw the overwhelming majority of his own men cheering and shouting approval, he knew he could not resist.

This Kolpak had the ability to reach and touch that common center of idealism and honor in all men, that deep recess of hope and aspiration the Russians called *duchinka*, the innermost soul. By the end of the speech, Isaac didn't even realize he had been moved to tears and he didn't even mind when the press of the crowd forced him off his perch on the pile of bricks. He was swept off and pulled along by the men; but he felt, somehow, part of the commotion and celebration.

Later that evening in front of a giant fire, Kolpak danced while the men drank. He danced with the Ukrainians, whirling about and leaping with a peasant's joy. Then, he kept dancing when some Georgians and Carpathians from the Polish city of Tarnopol stomped into their native steps. He could leap into the air with his legs outstretched, touching fingers to toes, combining a certain grace with rugged strength.

Through the night the festivity continued, with everyone celebrating the new unity. The house was turned into a feasting hall with food and drink from everywhere. There was Kolpak's favorite drink, *Gorilka*, a vodka seasoned with red pepper, along with *kvas*, a drink of fermented wild radishes and bread. There was *shashlik* broiling on open spits next to Polish sausages, and hours upon hours of toasts and more dancing.

Isaac was overwhelmed by the energy and fury of the celebration. He wandered about, smiling and shaking hands with strangers until a flushed and intoxicated Pietka grabbed and brought him to the side of Kolpak himself. Practically pushing the young man into the Russian commander, Pietka shouted, "Here's the best damn cook and doctor you can find anywhere!" Kolpak looked at Isaac's young, worn face and saw the vitality in his eyes, the warmth in his smile. "Whoever you are, my young soldier, I welcome you. We need everyone—cooks, doctors, the strong and the lame."

"Lame?" Pietka broke in. "Why, my friend is fast. He is faster than anyone. Like a lightning bolt. Like a flea from DDT." Kolpak laughed and took Isaac's shoulders with both hands.

"If you're that fast, we can use you in demolition. We need

quickness and brains. What's your name?"

Isaac, half-red with embarrassment and flushed with anger at Pietka, stammered for a moment, then blurted out, "Sergei. They call me Sergei."

"Well, Sergei, welcome to Kolpak's Brigade."

Later that night, Isaac noticed Wasic sitting down with Kolpak's men, going over supply drops and targets. By morning everyone seemed bleary-eyed, sick, or still drunk, except for Kolpak. He came out of the house looking as fresh and energetic as ever. He was followed by Wasic and Pietka, who both looked ashen and white, obviously staggered and drained by a night of carousing. But Kolpak didn't seem to notice and spoke to them as he walked briskly towards the truck. "You have your demolition squad, then. Right? Get one of the nurses to go with your team." When he saw Isaac, Kolpak smiled. "Ah...our bright, fast flea. In two weeks, Sergei, I'll have you blowing up trains. Two weeks. I promise." When he turned to confirm further plans with Wasic and Pietka, he saw they had wandered off to sleep. Shrugging off the sight of two of his soldiers stumbling off to sleep in the middle of a briefing, he went on, patting Isaac on the shoulder as he passed, conferring with the women in the nurse's truck and a Russian officer. Once more, Isaac noticed the nurse who had caught his eye the night before. She wore a dark, thin scarf over her brown hair and the drab padded jacket of the Russian partisan. He watched her as she spoke to Kolpak, nodding and smiling. Then Kolpak pointed to Isaac and left. The other Russian officer, Jasha, took the nurse by her arm and brought her over to where Isaac was standing. For a moment Isaac felt like he wanted to vanish or simply collapse in a drunken stupor. The Russian saluted Isaac and introduced himself. "I've been assigned to coordinate your group. My name is Jasha. Yours, I'm told, is Sergei." Isaac nodded. "Good. We have good men in this group, I hear." The nurse stood by

Jasha's side silently, obediently. But she kept staring at Isaac, as if she had remembered his face. "Oh yes, Kolpak has assigned us a nurse. Her name is Ducia and she is the best nurse around, I assure you, and a great barber, to boot."

Ducia smiled at Isaac, silently. "We've seen each other, haven't we?" Isaac nodded, shyly turning away. "I thought so." She held out her hand and Isaac took it. For a moment, he squeezed it a bit too hard, too affectionately, feeling a strange new surge of possessiveness as he touched her. "Nice meeting you, Sergei." Then she returned to her truck leaving Isaac spent and exhausted.

Later that same morning Kolpak performed his first miracle. He had assigned Jasha and another Russian, Alosha, to Isaac's group. Alosha was the demolition expert whose face served his profession well with its crooked, flat nose broken many times by exploding metal; gnarled, bushy eyebrows with fleshy scars burned into them; and skin pitted and creviced by shrapnel and fire. He had no rank and neither had Jasha, since Kolpak did not believe in the false hierarchy of military titles. Each man earned his rank from the men he led. With Jasha there was no need for titles. He looked like a leader, taller than Stepan with long, powerful legs and a strong, aggressive gait that also set the pace in any march. Like Stepan, he could probably rule by force and brute strength alone, but he tried under Kolpak's command to earn the respect and trust first. With Wasic and Novak still aching from the celebration and resentful of these strange new leaders, it wasn't easy.

Jasha indicated that there was an expected supply drop for the group in a few hours. He went over the coordinates and the timing, but Wasic and Novak listened half-heartedly, still disgruntled and suspicious.

"A plane will find us in these woods, in the middle of the marshes and drop gifts from the sky? Crazy! Where is this Kolpak? He must think we're crazy." Wasic sputtered and turned away. Novak followed.

Jasha tried to persuade. "Look, we have to be there by the afternoon if we are to receive..."

Wasic turned and muttered, "No one cared where we were or what we did for a year. Not you! Not this Russian Kolpak. No one! So don't tell me where I have to be. Don't tell any of us!"

Isaac tried to wake Pietka, still asleep in a crumple of blankets and clothing. But Pietka still couldn't move, so sodden and drenched with *Gorilka, kvass* and Moldavian wine. He knew that Pietka could help, but his friend just mumbled incoherently.

Meanwhile Jasha, holding back his temper, crunched the map in his fist and followed Wasic, intent on getting his agreement. Each step he took towards Wasic, however, appeared a gesture of threat and intimidation. Wasic, even with the aftermath of a drunken stupor clouding his instincts, moved his hand towards the automatic pistol in his belt.

At that moment, Kolpak appeared. He somehow sensed the confrontation and quickly stepped in.

"Listen, Wasic," Kolpak spoke quietly, "I know you lost a good man recently. The one called Stepan. No one can take his place. But if he was here and he was still leading you, do you think he'd turn his back on food and ammunition? It's all yours for nothing. It will drop from the skies if all goes as planned. And your only task is to be there to receive it. I don't think Stepan or Novak here or even you, Wasic, can deny that's a good bargain. Take everything. If you don't want to join us in our struggle, take whoever agrees with you, all the supplies you need, and all the good fortune you require, and we will part friends. But first we all need supplies. Right? Just a gift from heaven. What do you say?"

And with that Kolpak put his hand out. Wasic was totally outmaneuvered. He even felt a sudden bond of trust and shook Kolpak's hand, almost without thinking. "Wonderful. You know the Nazis call us all Kolpakniks, after me. Don't disappoint those fascist bastards. Burn their breeches off, in my name."

Then Kolpak snapped his fingers, ordered Jasha to prepare for travel and handed him the communication from Moscow indicating the supply planes had already taken off and were on target for the drop.

Isaac had to drag Pietka to his feet, and with the new recruits from Russia, Lithuania, Kiev, and the Ukraine, they all started their march towards the gifts from heaven. In the back of the long column of these new Kolpakniks, Ducia followed.

Towards late afternoon, near a meadow swept in high grass, the miracle occurred. Instead of begging villagers or robbing farmhouses or stealing from the marketplace, they watched as an American B-17 broke through the clouds briefly, dipped, and veered away, leaving a momentary tear in the clouds. Suddenly a great flock of parachutes opened like flowers in the air. It was perfectly timed and the cloth blossoms floated down into the meadow carrying crates and bundles just as promised. Wasic was stunned. He just watched as some of the men rushed to cut the parachutes loose and drag them into cover, while others hauled the crates back to temporary camp.

That night, along with ammunition and new weapons, Kolpak's brigade had American corned beef from cans torn open with bayonets. They also ripped open carton after carton of Pall Mall cigarettes. Everyone was smoking. Even Isaac was compelled to try his first cigarette and coughed his way through, pretending it was second nature to him.

The group had swollen to thirty with many new faces. Then Isaac noticed, by a small fire near the perimeter of the camp, the nurse Ducia and Jasha, stretching out his lanky legs next to her. It was clear that the new leader had laid claim to her. Trying to ignore the sight, Isaac turned back to his cigarettes. Lighting up again, he smoked with a gallant flourish, coughing only when he inhaled, while he secretly wished he had been born two feet taller and four feet broader. He sighed, took a deep breath, and began to cough uncontrollably from the cigarette. Angrily he threw down the butt, snubbed it out with his boot, threw the pack back into the pile of cartons and crawled into his bedroll. No cigarette or Russian commander could change his destiny. Though beset by unfamiliar feelings of jealousy and sensual longings, Isaac finally fell asleep. It would be a sound and deep sleep, his first night as a partisan and the first night he ever struggled with love.

CHAPTER SEVEN
DEMOLITION AND DUCIA

He was picked to blow up trains because he was the smallest and the quickest. What had been a burden to him in the past was now an advantage. A few others, including Novak, were chosen as well. For two days, Alosha, with the notched and pulverized nose, demonstrated the proper use of demolitions. He carried with him carefully—and stored delicately—stick after stick of dynamite; he also carried the soft putty and the fuses for insertion.

He demonstrated to the four men how to tie the sticks together, how to insert the short fuse, sealing it with putty. Then he brought them to a railroad track. Checking his schedule, he felt assured the track would be empty for at least two hours, so he went through the motions of blowing up a train.

First, he climbed up the siding. The four men followed him. At the top, he checked his watch against the schedule and began, placing the dynamite carefully between the rails and the wooden ties so that the train wheels could strike a portion of the dynamite if the fuse failed. Then with a hypothetical train approaching, he pretended to light the fuse and quickly slid down the embankment, running towards the cover of the forest. Each man went through the actions once, rehearsing silently in the insect buzz and gentle hum of a late afternoon.

The lesson was simple. Everything was timing. You timed the fuse to go off as the engine passed over the dynamite. You timed your departure from the rails so that you can escape detection and possible injury. The fuse was deliberately short, no more than half a minute. It was clear that the train was more important than the partisans carrying out the action. With a short fuse, the man was forced to wait until it was almost too late and the train was bearing down on him. In that way he could visually judge the time remaining.

If done right the engine would explode and set off a sequence of minor explosions from its own boiler, crumpling and derailing all the other cars. Since these German trains were speeding back from the Russian front, carrying captured armaments, including tanks and artillery pieces, food, and even cattle, along with priceless treasures, their destruction crippled Germany on their western front and demoralized them in their retreat from Russia.

The night before the first action, Isaac sat alone, away from the men, holding a bundle of dynamite in his hand, wrapping it and unwrapping, checking the fuse, resetting the putty. The sticks sat in his lap like some precious infant. Over and over, Isaac rehearsed the ritual, looking down at the dynamite in its simple paper innocence and remembering how hard it was to decipher his brother's medical texts at first, but how simple it became after time. As he studied and restudied the bomb, Pietka came over, sullen and restless. He looked down at Isaac and reacted, "Damn Bolsheviks!"

"What? What are you talking about? You never ate so well, Pietka!"

"Don't you see, Sergei. They don't really give a bedbug's ass about you. Look. The short fuse. They expect you to blow up with the damn train."

"It's a necessity. For timing. Too long a fuse and we all get sloppy."

"They don't care!"

"It'll all work out. I'll be perfect."

"It's only a few seconds."

"Pietka, you dumpling brain, I changed nationalities in a few seconds. You remember. I'm fast as a flea."

Pietka nodded, started away, stopped and faced his friend one more time, impulsively candid, "One other . . . . Listen, I see you looking at that nurse . . . what's her name?"

"Ducia."

"Don't. She's Jasha's girl. Even Novak might get in line for her. There are understandings about this. Stop even thinking."

"What are you talking about?"

"Don't even think about it. It's worse than that damn bomb in your lap. There are understandings."

Pietka shook his head in frustration and left, leaving Isaac to think even harder on the matter. He looked towards the new shelter built that afternoon to house a temporary headquarters for Jasha, and for Kolpak when he visited on his rounds. It had been constructed quickly by men excavating with shovels into the side of a small slope, then building a roof of short timbers and branches, and shoring up the dirt walls with more timbers and rocks. It looked like a lean-to or a shed buried into the side of a hill, and on the roof they could lay dirt and grass to camouflage it from the air. Inside the shelter Isaac could see the shadow of Jasha as he worked on an improvised table in candlelight.

Outside tending the fire was Ducia, cooking a large kettle of soup for the men. It had been Isaac who brought her the wild dill a few hours before to season the broth and the fragrance of the soup sweetened the very air around the camp. In the shadows, he watched as Ducia turned to talk to Jasha, then walked back into the shelter. She would live there now, with Jasha at her side. That was the understanding and there was nothing Isaac could do about it.

The next day, Alosha gave him his assignment and brought

him to the edge of the woods. Beyond, about a half kilometer away, were the tracks. Isaac checked the schedule with Alosha once more. His target was a shipment of cattle from the farms around Kiev and some undisclosed armaments. As Alosha reviewed the details, he never smiled. His lips always seemed parched and cracked beneath the tufts and curls of his thin beard. His voice, as well, was roughly hewed, cut from bitter stone, and offered little comfort. Isaac took in all he could, looked out towards the grass and brush, and beyond, the distant embankment where the train siding stood. Just as he was about to leave, Alosha abruptly shoved a silver timepiece into Isaac's hand. He said nothing, but Isaac knew it was a personal possession and the gesture filled him with a sense of faith and even a degree of optimism.

He checked Alosha's timepiece, then rushed across the field in a crouching position, the dynamite and fuses tucked away carefully in a rucksack across his shoulders. When he got to the edge of the tracks, he crawled between them. In the blistering heat, he quickly unpacked his explosive, lodged the bundles of dynamite between the wooden ties and the tracks, then inserted the fuse, sealing it with the soft putty. Now he waited, checked for his matches, checked his timepiece, and went on waiting. He crawled alongside the tracks, his legs dangling down the siding. In that position, he could listen for vibrations as well as feel them with his hand. In the distance, the tracks wavered like quicksilver in the heat of day. He checked for his matches again, then put his ear to the ground. He remembered that trick from reading Zane Grey and James Fenimore Cooper. Trackers or Indians could hear the approaching hooves miles away by listening to the earth. But he heard nothing. He knew he could not light the fuse until the engine was no more than thirty seconds away.

Sometimes, Alosha had warned, his fuse did not function

properly and then the man would have to retrieve the bundle if the train did not set it off. That was the most dangerous act of all since the dynamite or the fuse could suddenly malfunction once again and some small instability could set the bomb off in your face. He had been warned as well about the Nazis' use of water sprinklers in the front of the trains. It was thought that wetting certain stretches of track was done to saturate the fuse and dynamite and avoid demolition. There was so much to anticipate.

Probably Pietka was right. Nobody cared whether he lived or died. Maybe that was why the fuse was so short. But Isaac had stopped depending on others for survival a year ago. Except for Pietka, no one really cared. He tried not to think of Ducia and whether she even gave him a minute's thought. How wonderful it would be if Ducia worried, if Ducia waited, if she felt anything. He thought in a dark moment, *Who would mourn me? There would be nothing, no ceremony, no marking, no record. As if I never existed.* He took a deep breath and dwelled once again on the seconds ahead, leaving the hours and days for others. He was used to peering down the precipice and missing the fall by seconds each time.

He checked Alosha's timepiece, then listened once again. There was something, a distant throb, a soft rumble. Maybe it was a train. He felt a rush of nervous heat engulf his neck and cheeks. Then his throat tightened, and his stomach suddenly ached. He felt the track. There was still no vibration. So he went on waiting.

Like so much he had experienced in these months of the war, this, too, was not the adventure he had imagined as a boy. It did not seem noble or glorious, like all the heroes in Sir Walter Scott's novels. It did not even challenge one's sense of history or honor, like the struggle of heroes in Tolstoy or Stendhal. It was all too real and exact. He faced the mortality of it all like some brute creature would. If you lived, some other predator would take a bite out of you on another day; if you died, you were done with your enemies, at last.

Then he drifted back to thoughts of her, the dark babushka, the brown eyes, the smell of that wild dill soup. She was no maiden waiting for a knight. If he returned behind a shield or on top of it, it made no difference to her.

He suddenly stopped musing. There was a sound. He heard it: a distant shudder and clack. He touched the tracks. A slight vibration. It was happening. He quickly clambered back to his position between the tracks, checked the bundle of dynamite one more time, checked the fuse, checked his matches. He worried over the proper angle of the sticks so that the wheels could strike it and set off an explosion if the fuse failed. Then, he looked at the timepiece. The train was late. But that was usual. He knew it was coming.

Now the tracks were clacking audibly and he could feel the ties jumping slightly. In the distance, he saw a curl of smoke above the heat-shimmer rising from the metal tracks and turning the distant horizon into a blur of molten metal. The puff of smoke grew darker. It was time.

He swung over the side of the tracks, his feet dangling down the embankment, and he pulled out his matches. Pebbles rolled down the siding as he dug in his toes to get a better position on the dynamite. One last time, he felt the tracks. The metal rang and whistled under his palm. There was no time left. He struck the match, realized his hand was shaking, grabbed his wrist with the other hand to steady it, and lit the fuse. It quickly caught, smoldered, sparked and began to burn down. At that instant, he pushed back from the tracks and rolled down the siding, hit the ravine at the bottom and began to run. He figured he had twenty seconds left.

He sprinted across the field without turning back even when

he could hear the train hissing and clattering close by. By the middle of the field, he stumbled, fell to his knees and started up again. There were no more than ten seconds left and the train roared as if it was following him at his heels. Nearing the edge of the woods and with seconds left, he fell to the ground and held his arms about his head, anticipating the explosion and concussion. The sound of the train with its scrape and screech seemed on top of him. He counted one, two, then waited. First, there was a muffled boom, followed by a louder explosion. The second was as loud as a thunderstorm overhead; it shook the ground and vibrated in the air above his head. Then he heard a loud hiss and the crunching twist of metal. Another explosion and distant sounds, like screams or maybe the whine of animals. Then silence, with only the hiss of steam from the cracked broiler. The tension had numbed his body and it was only at this point he realized he had been covered by a shower of metal sparks and flying debris. His back and arms were cut and bleeding. There were dark scorch marks across his left forearm, and the pain became apparent for the first time. He quickly turned, looked in the distance to see his handiwork.

It was a violent picture. The engine had buckled in two, the long cars behind it had derailed and had crunched together like so many accordions, spilling their contents all about. Fire ripped through the roof of the engine and the two cars behind it. Puffs of smoke and fire scattered all about the field. He had turned the meadow into a hellish pit. Even with his pain, he was transfixed by the sight of all this destruction. Then he noticed dazed and moaning cattle wandering all about the siding and in and out of the wreck. He could see soldiers limping about trying to herd the animals away from the wreck. Some beasts had panicked and were in full gallop smashing against the wreck with their heads, butting it over and over. Other cattle ran at the soldiers or trampled through the field towards the forest.

Still stunned and fascinated, Isaac noticed bits of uniform and hats and medals all about, blown clear from the wreck. So many, he wondered if the Nazis were shipping some unused medals back in disgrace after the ignominious defeat in Russia. Quickly scooping up some of the decorations, he started on his way back into the woods, running without a rest for ten minutes until he was clear of danger and free from detection.

A half hour later he found his way back to the brigade. Alosha saw him first and nodded solemnly, holding out his hand for the timepiece, which Isaac delivered. Then he patted Isaac on the cheek and walked away. Pietka saw him next and quickly ran over, and mussed his hair playfully, relieved he was alive. Wasic and Novak saw him but did not respond. Meanwhile Isaac, as was his custom and style in all the operations he had joined, emptied his pockets of the trinkets and treasures he had picked up. He spread them on a blanket and invited the camp to share. It was always his policy never to keep anything except necessities. In this way, he was safer; he was never envied and nothing he had was coveted by another. This time, however, he kept one piece hidden, a service medal made of silver in the form of the Maltese Cross. One of the men offered him a canteen of water, another offered him some cigarettes, which he refused. It was then that Jasha came over, congratulated him and then noticed his condition.

"You're bleeding all over."

"I didn't know."

"Get Ducia to look at it."

He looked down at his burnt shirt, the singes on his boots, the bleeding cuts on his arms. Somehow the pricking of the burns and the metal cuts excited him. As his pain became more acute, he felt more alive. It made no sense, except it justified his visit with Ducia even more.

As he walked to the dugout with its low-slung, earth-covered roof, he could see the other men—strange, new faces—smiling at him. Behind him he caught sight of a laughing Jasha going over a map with Wasic and Alosha. Business as usual. No one dwelled on success.

He walked into the darkened interior with the dusty sunlight pouring down between the muddy rafters. Ducia was working at a table, cleaning it off, her sleeves rolled up, her padded vest unbuttoned, her scarf off. The long, thick hair fell down to her shoulders.

"Jasha told me to see you."

Ducia looked up. Just for a moment, Isaac thought he saw more than just a courteous smile; he thought he saw joy.

"Sergei, you've done it."

"My first. It made a mess of my skin."

"My poor boy. Let me get you cleaned off."

As she sat him down on the same chair she used to cut men's hair and knead the bread, she brushed her arm across his cheek. When she tried to wind the cut with gauze, Isaac reminded her of the usefulness of certain leaves for packing open cuts. He pointed out the proper ointment to be utilized from the first aid kit and she, self-reliant and proud, showed him a more modern treatment and newer medicine she had picked up as a field hospital nurse on the Eastern Front.

For a few minutes, both of them argued gently about Isaac's treatment, then Ducia put her hand over his mouth and hushed him.

"Here, I am the nurse."

"But I was a medical . . . "

"You'll teach me a little at a time; maybe I can teach you . . ., Agreed?"

Each time her fingers accidentally touched his face or skin, or when her body rubbed next to his, he felt excited. He wanted so much to touch her as well, but the feelings confused him. And he was afraid she would never understand.

With great care, she cleaned and dressed his wounds. As she did, she asked him some questions about his life, obviously aware of rumors she had heard. She seemed most interested in his books and education and the refinement of home life. Though still hiding behind his Russian origin, Isaac transposed his family life and home into the Caucasus. It was clear Ducia longed for a world of luxuries, comforts, gentleness, and beauty.

By the end of her treatment, he wanted to confide in her and tell her who he really was. But he held back, realizing the impulse was based on nothing but the rapture he felt near her. In the dim, dusty half-light of the dugout, she seemed the most beautiful woman he had ever met. And most assuredly, she was a woman, not a girl. Clearly, she was older than Isaac and reportedly, she had been married at least once. He did not see her as some idealized and idolized goddess, but as a warm, earthy woman. He was as afraid of that image as he was attracted to it.

Just before he left, he remembered the medal in his pocket. Quickly he thrust it towards her.

"Ducia, this is for you . . . "

She took it, held it to a dim shaft of sunlight and looked back at Isaac. Her eyes, so dark and large in the shadows, seemed almost watery.

"You're very . . . kind . . . "

"Well, you saved my skin."

"With your help."

"Do you like it?"

She just smiled back, rolled the medal over in her hand, then taking his hand, she pulled him further back into the shadows, out of sight of everyone else, and kissed him on the cheek. Isaac did not know what was happening. Before he could kiss her back, or embrace her, she was by him and out the entrance, shouting to someone for some more potatoes. Isaac stood for a moment in the dark, smelling the rich, fertile underbelly of the scooped-out hill that made up the back of the shelter. The moist fragrance of soil and roots and cold stone made him dizzy. He steadied himself, then walked out and passed Ducia with a simple, friendly nod. So went the understanding.

CHAPTER EIGHT
THE EDDIES

Over the next few months, Isaac became a legend. He success-fully blew up fifteen trains and always brought back treasures to share with the whole camp. He never came back empty-hand-ed. Most of all, he never kept a thing for himself, whether it was a priceless Browning rifle or a tin medal.

Of the original four who started, Isaac was the only one still alive. Novak died months before on his fifth train when he mis-judged the explosion and caught a large piece of metal in his back, puncturing both lungs. Given his incredible record, Isaac was now known as "the miracle man." No matter what went wrong, it was well-known that Isaac would not return from an assignment until he had blown up some train. If the first train wet his dynamite down with water, or the fuse proved defec-tive, Isaac would not leave. He would reset the fuse or bundle new dynamite and wait until another train came by.

Even Pietka was impressed. "You know, bedbug, I think you enjoy almost blowing yourself up. You're either crazy or . . . in love." He would glance back in the direction of Ducia's dugout and grin back at Isaac. Only Pietka knew of Isaac's feelings, and he wouldn't dare tell anyone. When it came to the understand-ings about women in the camp, nothing had changed in spite of Isaac's new reputation.

When a new nurse, Soya, arrived, there was some scuffling between Wasic and others, but in the end Wasic claimed her as his woman. He had some authority and seemed capable of murdering anyone who opposed him.

Such arrangements and undertakings appalled Isaac, but he did not protest. Unlike the others, he did not see each new woman as a commodity. Granted, these were resourceful females capable of cooking, cleaning, and cutting hair along with their medical duties. They gave a man a certain sense of importance and status. But as Isaac had learned over the past months, a man could only claim his woman for her duties and services. Whatever other companionship that followed was outside the agreement. Ducia had made that very clear to Isaac during one of their conversations. It was almost as if she was reassuring him of her fidelity. Nevertheless, Ducia still belonged to Jasha, and this brigade of men was a closed and inflexible community. There was little room for jealousies and secret liaisons.

Still, Isaac would come to Ducia after each mission for medical treatment. He always managed to acquire some sort of cut or bruise to justify the visit. He sat with her in the shadow of the shelter and discussed medical histories he remembered from his brother's textbooks and patients. In return, Ducia would share stories about her days as a field hospital nurse.

Each visit grew longer and would always end with Isaac giving her the most precious part of his booty, whether it was a jeweled medal or a fancy can of caviar. He would save the best prize for her and she would take the gift and carefully store it in a large leather satchel which contained her barber supplies.

Even though Kolpak's men often moved their camps to follow the retreat of the German troops, there was always an attempt to set up some kind of sheltered dugout in which Ducia carried out her field duties and kept her prizes. During the winter, it was more difficult. They were often forced to sleep together in a large cave or, if at all possible, they would commandeer a house and use it as the bunkhouse for everyone. Otherwise, these earthbound dugouts became the main meeting place for Ducia and Isaac.

With each successive visit, they talked more and more about personal memories. Though Isaac still hid his Jewish past from her, he simply transposed his childhood house to some town near Mount Kazbek in Georgia and shared real incidences and memories. At first, Ducia seemed almost embarrassed to talk about herself. She imagined Isaac's life to be full of luxuries and culture. When he mentioned his mother's gilded mirror in the foyer or the great dining room table, Ducia sighed. Often, he would embellish his memories, adding another room to his house or a few more workers to the factory. But Ducia could not get enough of Isaac's image of western living. It was her ultimate dream to live in New York in a great building. Somehow, she had imagined the wealthy in New York living in mansions as big as office buildings.

So when Isaac talked of his mother, he flooded the dim interior of the shelter with radiant pictures of a refined woman, beautiful, talented, and highly cultured. Ducia always asked for more stories about his mother. She became the symbol of western life, the truly civilized modern woman. Isaac could not wait to talk more of his past. But sometimes, when he conjured up his family too vividly in words, he saw them new and alive and irresistibly attractive. That was when the sorrow returned, and he had to stop, choking back the tears. He was sure Ducia never knew how close he was to tears so many times in their meetings. It was at those moments of lament that Isaac came closest to telling Ducia everything. But each time he pulled back, each time he concealed the truth.

By the sixth and seventh visit, Ducia would spend more time washing the cuts and burns, and as she ministered him, her touch became more intimate and loving. Isaac was sure she was not simply the nurse in these moments. With the growing tenderness, Ducia also grew more trusting and soon, she began to share her personal history as well. It came out in short, tentative passages with no chronology or continuity. If she suddenly remembered her father, she would tell some fragment of memory with her family. If her days in the field hospital came back to her, she spent all the time on that period. But Isaac put it all together in his mind, carefully rearranging it until it all flowed as one piece.

He was certain of some kind of chronology near the end. She was born into a poor farming family who grew cabbages and carrots in the dusty clay of a small town in the province near Kiev. It was a drab and impoverished existence. Her memories of childhood were further embittered by stories of her father. He was an uneducated man, a true serf, who refused, in Ducia's words, "to better himself." When his crops failed or the money ran out or one of his children took sick, he blamed it first on his wife, then on the government, then on the Lord. Often, he would drink at a nearby tavern all through the week and return home violent and rebellious. It was then that Ducia, only six years old at the time, remembered brutality. The way he beat her mother with his fist and threw chairs and lifted whole tables over his head and smashed them against the wall. He would not touch Ducia, but rather take her to his side after his fury subsided and cry while he held her, confessing all his guilts and shortcomings into the ear of a six-year-old child. As Ducia put it to Isaac, "What could I do? I was his child and I always forgave him."

One day he didn't return from his week-long binge, and later, Ducia remembered, vaguely, some kind of funeral. It was never very clear, but she was sure he died far from home. Her mother kept at the farm, working day and night, and demanding the same devotion from Ducia. But by the time she was fourteen, Ducia dreamed of cities and America. She could not wait any longer and left her birthplace for good, traveling to Kiev.

In that rich and varied city, she found a place cutting men's hair and listening to their gossip. Somehow, it pleased her. She loved cutting the hair and loved being with men, listening to them talk.

Later as the war approached, she met her husband, Khludov, a poor postal clerk with a waxed mustache and a starched collar. "I swear, Sergei; I swear," she would say to Isaac, "I thought he was royalty, at least. Someone imperial. Some fine manners, it seemed. And he always splashed himself with some kind of rosewater."

She met him in front of a brilliantly lit opera house where an elegant party was going on and somehow she convinced herself that he had been a guest at this party and was leaving alone. That fantasy kept Ducia interested in this man. She dreamed of silver-edged invitations and fancy clothes. But of course, it was all wrong: the man, the age, the setting. She was chasing some fanciful image of czarist Russia. Khludov was no aristocrat. In fact, he was not even a gentleman.

Soon after the marriage, conducted in a drab office by the postal service, he insisted she work longer hours as a barber. Then he took the money she earned and spent it on more extravagance for his own vanity. As she spent longer at her work, he also grew more suspicious and jealous. Finally, he accused her of flirting with every man she met and insisted she quit her job. When she refused, he exploded and drew a pistol on her. Frightened and alone, she surrendered to his demand and spent months sitting in a small, cramped apartment, afraid to venture out without him, for fear that he would be waiting just to shoot her.

Finally, when Germany invaded Russia, Khludov was conscripted against his wishes and quickly transported up to the front. They insisted he shave his mustache and they confiscated his satchel full of eau de cologne and hair pomade. Ducia was relieved, but felt sad for her husband, knowing how vulnerable he would be in a world of unclean, slovenly men. "That's when I realized how little I knew about men," she confessed to Isaac during one visit. A week after he was sent into battle, she got a telegram back saying her husband had been decorated twice for bravery and was now recuperating in a field hospital for minor injuries. "Of course, I said to myself, he must have been a real killer with a gun." They would both laugh at the painful irony of it all. A week later, she received a letter indicating he was missing in action. It was then in her strange, almost penitent loyalty to men, that she decided to volunteer for field hospital service as a nurse and search for her husband.

While she tended the wounded on the Eastern Front, German paratroopers landed behind the lines, cutting her hospital off from the rest of Russia. She fled west towards Pinsk. It was in the marshes that she met Kolpak for the first time and fell under his charm. Once again, she worked for men, with men, and under men. "I should be tired of all of you. But there is always someone to surprise me. Always some new man." She never finished that thought.

In all of these conversations, Ducia and Isaac never grew bored of each other. Limited by the confinements of their partisan existence, they courted each other only in the dark of the dugouts with the daylight filtering weakly through the girders and the spill of dirt and gravel between the roof beams creating a constant backdrop to their increasingly intimate talks.

By the fifteenth visit, Isaac was frustrated by his lack of candor. He wanted to burst out and tell her as so many times before...and until he did, he felt he had no right to her love or her intimacy. It was on this last visit that he turned to her while she was gently applying ointment to a burn on his shoulder and whispered, "I have not been fair with you."

She stopped, stiffened, and looked at him curiously. "There

is something I must tell you. I should have told you before, but I was not sure." She was almost amused at Isaac's sudden solemnity. Then he told her everything he could about his real birthplace, about his Jewish upbringing, and finally, most painfully, he told her about the death of his parents and his escape. He did not hesitate once he started and he would not let Ducia interrupt until he was done.

She listened, standing very still, then moving towards the table where she kept her medical supplies. When he finished, she moved further away from him, back into the darker corner of the shelter. There she sat down, stunned, confused, and she began to cry. When Isaac moved toward her, she shook her head, telling him in a sobbing, broken voice to "Go, please, now. Leave now."

Isaac felt betrayed. He was suddenly very angry and humiliated, saddened and bewildered. He walked out convinced he would never speak with her again.

The next day a new officer, Golovan, appeared in the camp. He was reported to be a colonel in the Russian artillery. He wore a tight-fitting military uniform with all his medals and marched about with Jasha as if he was reviewing some crack battalion. Golovan carried a small, silver-handled pistol in his belt and often took it out, twirling it in his hands while he talked. After a few days of settling in, he ordered Jasha to let Ducia work for him. Since he outranked everyone, Jasha could not protest. Suddenly, Ducia was assigned to this rigid and regimented officer. In turn, Jasha approached Soya, the other nurse, and asked her to now report to his shelter. Once more, the arrangements changed according to the unspoken agreements between men. But Wasic had not been consulted. When he returned from a reconnaissance mission the next morning, he searched for his Soya. When she walked out of Jasha's dugout, he looked about, demanding from his comrades what had happened. Pietka tried to explain, but was pushed away. With each attempt at an explanation, Wasic grew more and more incensed. Finally, he threw down his traveling gear, picked up his Mauser automatic pistol, loaded it, and walked towards Jasha's headquarters.

Isaac watched from a distance, feeling somewhat detached from this ceremony of power. When Wasic reached Soya, he took her by the hand and started dragging her back to his area. Then Jasha, watching it all from his table, stepped outside and quietly but firmly warned Wasic, "I have need of some woman to assist me." Wasic kept walking. "Do you hear me, Wasic? I am telling you it is necessary for me to have Soya to report to me."

Then Wasic stopped and looked back at his superior, "We all have need of women, Jasha. Didn't Kolpak say we were all equal? Well, I have equal need."

At that, Jasha took out his Russian pistol with the long barrel and loaded the chamber as he talked, "If you wish to ignore my request, then we can settle it in the other way." Having loaded the pistol, he cocked the trigger back, pointing the barrel down. Wasic heard the click and snap of the gun. He stopped, dropped his grip of Soya and looked about. There was a sense of humiliation and fury in his eyes. No one, not a single comrade, would come to his aid. He knew that. He knew he would fight this alone. Suddenly, he felt betrayed as a man and sabotaged as a soldier by his own comrades. He looked at Soya and gave her a nod to return to Jasha. She rushed back, past Jasha and into the shelter. Then Wasic, feeling desperate and vengeful, asked, "Then where is Ducia? Have Ducia report to me!"

"We have a new officer, a man named Golovan. A Major," Pietka explained.

"I've been fighting side by side with all of you for over a year. Who is this Golovan? Here one day and we give him our women?"

With that, he awaited some kind of reply from the other men. When none came, Wasic grew ever wilder and walked towards a small clearing where a new dugout was to be built. He knew the Major would be comfortably accommodated in the shadow of his new dugout. When Wasic arrived, the Major was seated in a small folding canvas chair, having his hair cut by Ducia. She looked sullen and resigned. But when she saw Wasic, she stopped and backed away.

"What is this?" The Major saw the look on Wasic's face. "Who are you?" Wasic then walked up to Ducia, took her by the arm and pulled her down the short hill. The Major, with a linen cloth still around his neck, stood up indignantly. "You're crazy!"

Wasic seemed indifferent to the Major's accusation and continued to pull Ducia down the slope. But this time, it was the woman who protested. Ducia suddenly pulled away from Wasic, screaming, "I don't belong to you, to anyone!"

For a moment, Wasic was startled. To him, it was like his boots suddenly complaining about their treatment. He tried to smile weakly and convince Ducia this was the way things were arranged. But when he reached for her, she backed away. By this time, the Major had put on his tunic and was charging down the slope. Meanwhile, Jasha, with his own woman safely behind him, started down to mediate the next crisis. That was when Wasic panicked. He saw the entire brigade about to encircle and subdue him. He was besieged. It wasn't true of course, since most of the men simply left these kinds of struggles to the principal players, but Wasic saw ambush and defeat. He lunged for Ducia, took her by the neck, placing his gun to her head and then held her in the crook of his arm, threatening to kill her if anyone dared make a move.

The Major kept thundering forward in a military gait. The

closer he came, the more desperate Wasic seemed. He tightened his grip around Ducia's neck and pushed the pistol harder into her temple. Jasha saw how serious Wasic was and tried to keep the Major out of it. But the Major plunged ahead, convinced his rank alone would immunize him from any attack. He was simply going to take his woman back. Wasic pulled Ducia with him as he retreated. He was starting to sweat and his hand trembled in nervous anger. What he didn't see was Isaac quickly and silently circling around through the trees to come from behind. As soon as Ducia was threatened, something clicked inside of Isaac's head, and he sized up the best rescue route.

Just before the Major reached out to grab Ducia, Isaac rushed from behind. He grabbed Wasic's arm as he barreled into his back, knocking him off balance.

As Wasic fell, Ducia broke free and ran into the woods. When the Major tried to stop her, she slapped his face in defiance. By the time Jasha arrived, the crisis was over. Except for an embittered and vengeful Wasic, Jasha was sure the brigade could slowly return to its normal routine. He tried to talk to the spurned Wasic, but to no avail. All Wasic wanted was revenge on this brigade that had shamed him and assaulted his sense of honor. When Isaac tried to help Wasic up, he, too, was rebuffed. No one could touch him. He sat there for a while, then stood and wandered off alone.

While the Major grumbled about the disobedience, Jasha tried to explain. But it was Ducia who had been left alone by everyone. Isaac realized she had walked down towards the river, and he slowly, casually, started down in that direction.

The river near the camp was narrow, but swift and deep. It curved by a bank of high reeds, then opened up wider past a shore of white pebbles and large cool boulders. It was at that point that the river twisted around rocks and deep underwater springs. With all the confusion of currents and irregular bottoms, the river turned into a swirl of whirlpools and foaming rapids. The men called this part of the river, the eddies. It was there, sitting by the white pebbles that Isaac found her. He came into view, hesitated, waited for some response. With none, he decided to answer, "I just wanted to make sure you were all right."

She shook her head and Isaac started to walk back to camp.

"Isaac! Wait." Ducia had never called him Isaac before.

"Is there anything . . . "

"You understand what I feel."

"Of course. Perfectly. A human being is not chattel. You can't move a woman about like so many boots or rifles."

"It's not that. I accept the arrangement, most of the time. No. It's not that."

There was a pause. The river behind them bubbled and rushed, clashing and colliding into new whirlpools and white foam.

"You told me who you were . . . . You said, Isaac from this town. Rovno. Just like that."

"I was tired of pretending with you."

"You know, Isaac, the men I know never leave gifts just like that. They never tell me everything on their mind, just like that. In fact, they never share anything. They take. Roughly, always roughly."

"I didn't mean to burden you with my troubles."

"Isaac, you are a damn fool of a boy. I can see that. And I love you for it."

"You do?"

"I have to get back and finish the Major's haircut. There is a war on." As she went by him, she brushed her hand by his cheek, then kissed him. Isaac tried to kiss her back, taking her in his arms. But she pushed him away . "No, no, my sweet. Not now. Later. In two hours. Here. By the eddies." She left Isaac and returned to the Major, while Isaac wandered back slowly, dreaming of what she said, anxious and expectant.

He came back to the eddies half an hour early. By the river's edge, he tried to wash up. It was not easy bathing in this war. No one dared to take off their clothing for fear someone would take them. Seldom did real baths ever occur. From time to time, Isaac would powder himself liberally with DDT just to keep his hairy body clean. In fact, Ducia would often mistake the DDT for some strange new cologne or perfume.

This time when he washed up quickly, he caught sight of his face in the pool. For a very long time, Isaac had avoided his own reflection, afraid to see a sick or dying face staring back. Leading over the quiet pool of water just before the eddies, he studied his face. He looked to see what Ducia saw. In the translucent flicker of the water, he recognized the face. It was fuller than he had ever remembered it, less haggard, more weathered and worn. A certain knowing of maturity in the lines of the cheeks. The peaked, receding hairline gave him an air of intellectuality, while his simple, chunky nose gave his face the openness of a child. When he smiled into the water, he could see the broken tooth and the chipped molar. This was the Isaac Ducia had asked to see again. Not the Isaac of Rovno, who was a sweet, gullible boy. This Isaac was a man in Kolpak's brigade, a demolition expert and a wary individual. Wary and worn. Then, he threw a rock at the water, breaking up his reflection. He tried to flatten down the bushy hair growing up from the top of his head. As he patted his hair down, Ducia came up from behind a tree. She was watching all the time.

"You look wonderful, Isaac. Wonderful." She held out her hand and he took it. Then, she led him towards the brush just beyond the eddies. There she sat down on the ground and again held out her hand to Isaac. He took it and kneeled beside her. Gently, he took her face in his hand and kissed her. The she drew him down to her side, quietly and patiently leading him through the movements of love. It would not be the wild and sensual abandon that Isaac imagined. Not here, in the midst of war in a partisan outpost. Instead, they removed no clothing, not even their boots. She simply unbuttoned her shirt, loosened her pants buckle, then turned to Isaac, guiding him through the economy of this austere consummation. Taking his hand, she moved it through her blouse and let his fingers touch and explore her breasts. With a gentle movement of her hips, she slid under his body, while she adjusted the snaps and buttons of her pants, and with the other hand loosened his waist and buttons.

Isaac struggled and twisted, but he did not force anything. In spite of the wild pitch of excitement he felt through his body, he held back, trying against the urging of his flesh, to be in perfect harmony with her preparations.

Finally, with her hand directing him, he was with her, fondling, caressing and pushing inside her. Ducia rose to his movements, and each aroused the other in perfect pitch. In spite of all the confining clothes and rough fabrics; in spite of the uneven terrain and the pinch of the boots as they rolled ever-so-slightly about; in spite of all the limitations, they opened up completely to each other. Ducia forgot who was master and who was teacher by the end, biting at his lip and pushing him down harder against her body until they both felt spent.

At the end, they lay side by side, their clothing still on, the boots still in place, and listened to the nearby waters rushing in circles. When Isaac turned his face towards Ducia to say something, she kissed him. There would be no more conversation.

Even as they prepared to return to camp, adjusting their clothing and hugging each other once more, there was little talk. Ducia touched her fingers to his lips and left first so that no one would suspect. Isaac waited, his mind and heart racing together in some kind of joyous dance. Then, he followed.

Two days later, Isaac came to the Major's half-completed dugout. He asked to have Ducia give him a haircut. The Major grunted, glaring at this slip of a man with barely enough chest and shoulders to lug a rifle. Almost amused by the slightness of his build, the Major consented.

During the haircut, Ducia moved the clippers and scissors almost sensually about his head, barely cutting off any hair, just going through the motions for appearance sake. But they barely spoke. It was as if they had reached the end of everything they could tell each other. They were speechless. There was only love left. Before Isaac left, he looked up at her longingly. She whispered, "The eddies in two hours." Their conversation was complete.

CHAPTER NINE
THE CLEARING

Isaac couldn't sleep. He walked outside in the early morning dark, his Mauser rifle slung over his shoulder. Ducia had promised to see him this day, at dusk, near the eddies. He had not been alone with her by the river in over a month and a half. So much had happened since then, he was desperate to feel her near him.

It was early November 1944 and the German army had already retreated west of Kolpak's Brigade. Isaac was sure that Kolpak would soon begin disbanding his brigade and send the fighters and the nurses back to their countries, their homes, and their waiting families and friends.

Except Isaac knew he had no home left, no country, no family, and no friends waiting for him. Only Ducia. He was sure of her. She would wait for him, tonight at the eddies and afterwards. Even in her Russian village, she would surely wait. But could he ever come to her?

He couldn't wipe away the memory of what happened two days ago that convinced him even more of the suspicion and murderous hate awaiting him if he tried to make his way through Poland and Ukraine to Russia and Ducia.

Two days ago, the morning started out as quiet and uneventful. Isaac was standing on patrol with Pietka, their rifles strapped over their shoulders as usual.

Suddenly, a boy, a young teenager at most, stumbled out of the forest into Kolpak's camp. The boy's shoulder and arm were bloody from gunshot wounds; his oversized shirt, soaking wet, was streaked with mud and blood. When Isaac saw the boy, he thought he looked familiar, like so many local boys he once knew in Rovno.

Isaac didn't feel the boy was a threat and kept his rifle strapped to his shoulder. But Pietka stood by, his rifle pointed, ready to shoot the boy if Isaac was threatened.

The young boy approached Isaac, his feet dragging, his face gaunt and mud-splattered. He glanced nervously at Pietka with his gun pointed at him. "I . . . I have no guns. Tell your friend. See." He turned his pockets in his torn, stained pants inside out to show Pietka he was defenseless.

Isaac raised his hand to reassure him. "It's all right."

Then all at once, the boy began to talk, breathlessly, rapidly, his voice stuttering from fatigue and fear, as if there was not enough time to tell his whole story. "I was in hiding . . . Do . . . do you believe me? With . . . with my brother and cousins. That's all . . . that's all left of my family. My brother knew . . . he knew what German soldiers do to people like us. . . . Made . . . made us hide." He looked nervously at Pietka who still kept his rifle pointed at him, then whispered to Isaac in a terrified voice. "Do you kill Jews here too? Is it the same here?"

"Don't say anything more," Isaac pleaded. "Just say you were attacked by the Germans. That's all. Just say that."

The boy started to cry. Isaac put a finger to the boy's mouth to keep him quiet, but he sobbed, choked in his tears and whispered. "It wasn't German soldiers. No! It was a farmer we knew . . . just outside our village . . . a farmer . . . and his sons. We came . . . came to his farm for food. . . . Just food. But they attacked us. The farmer and his sons. . . . Not soldiers. . . . Neighbors . . . our neighbors. . . . And they attacked us."

Isaac pleaded. "That's enough! No more stories."

The young boy shook his head and kept talking, gasping between sentences, "One of the farmer's sons . . . he came at my brother . . . from behind . . . from behind with a stone. . . . " The boy, growing weaker, went down on his knees. "Hit him again and again." He pounded the ground with his fist, "Like he was nothing. Like his life was nothing."

On his knees, the boy kept on talking, tearfully, frantically. Isaac tried to stop him but he kept on. "And then . . . then they started shooting . . . . Went after my cousins . . . . Why? Why? We had no guns. . . . Shooting at all of us . . . . I ran . . . . What could I do?" He coughed, tears streaked his face. "I ran . . . ran . . . so much shooting . . . . Don't remember getting shot . . . . " He tried to lift his wounded arm, but the pain was too much for him to move it even just a little. "Ran . . . hid . . . in the marshes . . . . Afraid to make a sound . . . for days . . . . Afraid . . . . Not a sound . . . . Nothing." It was too much. He passed out, collapsed, sprawled on the ground.

Isaac lifted him gently and carried him to Ducia's dugout for treatment. When he carried the boy in, he saw that Ducia was giving Major Golovan a haircut. She looked somber, pale, and moved slowly around the Major with her scissor. Isaac could see she was not well. She had not looked like herself for weeks.

Isaac put the young boy down on the only long table in the dugout. Ducia saw the concern for the boy in Isaac's eyes and stopped cutting hair. It was then the Major responded with an upraised arm. "What is this? Who have we here? He's not one of us."

Isaac answered with a lie, "The German soldiers killed his family and they tried to kill him."

The Major stood up; the cloth around his neck covered with strands of his hair fell to the ground. "What is he talking about? Didn't you listen to Kolpak? Our troops captured over 60,000 filthy Nazis in Korsun months ago. The rest of those Nazi bastards are on the run, halfway to Berlin. What do you think, they stopped running just to attack this boy? Nonsense! He means nothing to them. He's lying. Just a trouble maker!"

He motioned to Ducia to finish his haircut, but she was already examining the boy's bullet wound, ordering Isaac to bring what little ointment they had left from a Red Cross first-aid kit that came with the last supply drop not far from the camp. The Major's face tightened. He glared at Isaac, then at Ducia. "Let Soya take care of this one. I need you." Ducia was too busy to react. She felt the boy's wrist to check his pulse, then his forehead. She turned to Isaac, "Burning up with fever. Dehydrated. In shock from loss of blood." She worked frantically over the young boy, cleaning the wound as best she could, trying to force water down his throat. The boy started to chatter and shake like he was freezing cold.

"Did you hear me, Ducia?" The Major shouted. "Get Soya. Leave the boy to her. Now!"

Ducia, half-listening, covered the boy with the two blankets Isaac brought her, then wiped his feverish forehead with a wet rag. The Major grabbed Ducia's arm to drag her from the boy, but Ducia would have none of it. She pulled her arm away. "Cut your own hair!" she snarled at him.

The Major was stunned. He backed away, tense, angry, not used to being upbraided by anyone, least of all a woman. But he was chastened and left the dugout, grumbling.

An hour later, in spite of Ducia's constant ministrations, the boy started to shudder in her arms as she held his head up to get him to drink another sip of water, then stiffened, then stopped shaking, stopped sweating, stopped breathing. He was gone.

He was to be buried without ceremony in the woods. Isaac and Pietka volunteered to carry the body and dig a shallow grave. Ducia followed them. When the boy was settled in the ground, the men starting shoveling until he was covered by a mound of earth. Then Isaac spread leaves and pine needles over the mound in the hope that no animal would disturb the grave.

The work completed, Pietka left, leaving Ducia alone with Isaac. But Isaac felt he could not leave the boy without some act of reverence. "Ducia, you have to know. He was a Jew; a Jew murdered by his own villagers. I can't just leave him here without some...." He shook his head, unable to find the words. She looked at Isaac, saw the grief in his eyes, and understood. She quickly performed her own act of reverence: three fingers on her forehead, then on her heart, then her right and left shoulder—the sign of the cross she learned as a Russian Orthodox child.

Finished, she stood silently while Isaac, shuffling slightly in the ritual rocking back and forth, recited the Kaddish to himself. When he stopped, he turned to her, took her hand and kissed it. She smiled sadly, caressed his cheek and told him, "I must see you. Before I...." She hesitated to finish the sentence. Her eyes watered. Isaac saw clearly how tired and weary she had become. For a moment, her mouth quivered as if she was suddenly stricken with some unbearable pain. She leaned over, took a deep, agonized breath, and when she looked up at him again, he realized how pale she had become. He took her hand and drew her close to him.

"Ducia, love, is there anything I...?"

But Ducia shook away his words, "Not now. By the eddies. The day after tomorrow. At dusk. Promise." He wanted to embrace her, hold her close to him, but she turned away and left him alone, standing over the boy's grave.

A slight wind sighed through the branches of the sunlit trees. Isaac sighed as well, then looked down at the grave, the image of a stricken Ducia crowding his thoughts. Then, he looked up at the sky hidden by the veil of leaves. In that moment, bathed in the patchwork radiance of the forest, Isaac remembered suddenly how, as a young boy, he would stand in rapture in the center of Rovno's Gochov Synagogue with the sun streaming through the towering stained-glass windows, filling the air around him with a myriad of colors. On one side, the window depicted the Tree of Knowledge with its seductive, bright red apple; and on the other window the Tree of Life, in a garden full of lush foliage and billowing flowers.

Now, standing beneath a canopy of leaves and sky, Isaac sensed a similar kind of rapture, not unlike the feeling he once had as a child bathed in the glow of Gochov's windows.

It was then Isaac realized he didn't even know the boy's name. Just like that, the young boy had disappeared from the earth, nameless as if he had never lived. The boy's words about his brother came back to him: "Like his life was nothing, like he was nothing." It was not right. It was not just. He was about to leave; then instinctively, he reached for a small stone and placed it on the boy's grave, a small, simple act of remembrance. It was more than he was ever was able to do for his family and his fellow Jews lying unmarked in their brutal grave. He took a deep breath and turned back to the partisan camp.

Now, two days later, the memory of the boy and the image of his lonely grave still haunted Isaac. He tried to keep his mind on his meeting with Ducia this evening. He looked up and saw the sky brightening into a cool, October dawn.

Pietka, coming up from behind, startled him with a gentle tap on his shoulder. "Sergei, Kolpak wants to see us now."

As they walked towards Kolpak's quarters, Pietka grabbed Isaac's arm suddenly. "Sergei, I'm worried."

Isaac looked at him. " About what?"

"Kolpak's going to send us all home soon. Some of our comrades have left already."

Isaac nodded. "I heard. I know."

"I don't think it's safe."

"For who?"

"For you . . . ." For the moment, Pietka forgot Isaac's real name, his Jewish name. "For you . . . Sergei . . . . For you."

"Don't worry about me."

"I'm your friend. Believe me. Trust me. You will be a target. People like Wasic, people like that who don't know anything except how to hate people like you, they're everywhere. They're all that's left."

"People like me?"

"You know what I mean."

Isaac stopped walking. "This is not a good time for this."

But Pietka kept at it. "You saw what happened to that poor boy. Just because . . ."

"Just because . . . ?"

"You know what I'm saying."

" I know. No more, Pietka. Please."

"You saw the fear in the boy's face. It wasn't the German army after him. It wasn't soldiers who killed him. It was neighbors. Countrymen. Our countrymen. I heard him. 'Neighbors', he called them. In every town, in every village, they will try and hurt you. It will be the same everywhere. I know it. You know it."

"Why are you telling me all this?"

"I know we will be going back soon. We will be returning home. But you can't. You mustn't. Not now. Maybe in time. But not now. Just because . . ."

Isaac raised his voice angrily. "Because I'm a Jew?"

"Not so loud! Even some of our Russian comrades here can't be trusted."

"Is that it, Pietka?" Isaac asked softly. "Because of what I am?"

"For some, it's enough. Trust me." Pietka stopped. He bit his fist, as if he was swallowing his words. "I'm sorry." Pietka was

126

almost in tears.

Isaac put his arm around Pietka. "I know." They stood together at the entrance to Kolpak's headquarters.

Kolpak's roof of wooden planks had been covered over after each rainstorm with a matting of dirt and grass, though the morning sun still streamed through cracks. There was a heavily marked map spread over his table with Kolpak standing behind it. In the corner, his assistant, Mikhail, was busy on a radio transmitter, listening with earphones. Isaac could hear the faint crackling sound of static humming in Mikhail's ear.

Kolpak smiled. "Comrades, I know you've already heard of the glorious victories of our Soviet Army." Pietka smiled. Isaac nodded in agreement. "Sergei. You, especially, must understand that is the reason we have not sent you out for months to disrupt a German train. Our Soviet Air Force has taken over your mission. You understand?"

Isaac nodded.

"So it's coming to that time when we can all return to our own people. Comrades, I know how closely you two have worked with Ducia, so you will understand why she is a special case and will leave first."

Isaac was puzzled. "A special case, sir? I don't know..."

"She is not well. I'm sure you have noticed her condition. She is in need of immediate medical care she can only receive in our Mother Russia. She will be evacuated by one of our transport planes as soon as we can coordinate the scheduled landing."

Isaac tried not to show any emotion, but his head was swirling with questions and concerns. "How much time...?"

"Soon. That is why I am asking you both to join us in helping clear a landing strip. As soon as we can clear the land, we will inform our pilot that we're ready. Can we do it by tomorrow, comrades?"

"Of course, Commander," Pietka replied. Isaac stood silent.

In the next few hours, a group of partisans, along with Isaac, Pietka, and Wasic, followed Major Golovan towards the heart of the white birch forest to a strip of land between the trees wide enough and long enough for a landing and take-off. They carried pickaxes and shovels.

In a few minutes, the clearing came into view. It was bordered on both sides by birches, shimmering white and brilliant in the afternoon sun. For a brief instant, Isaac was thrust back into his childhood. It was in such a setting his family would often spend an afternoon of picnicking, feasting, and singing. Isaac's heart ached with the memory. The unbroken line of the birch trees and the inviolable whiteness of their bark had always reminded the young Isaac of a sacred temple wall, guarding and preserving the sanctity of his family. But the memory quickly faded when he heard the Major shouting at him, "Get moving, Sergei! We've got work to do!"

The Major glared at Isaac while he set about his business. "You, Sergei and Pietka! Start clearing away the roots and the brush. Dig them out. The ground must be flat. Over there and there." The Major pointed to a part of the proposed landing strip that was overgrown with tangled brambles full of thorny spikes. Wasic and the rest were assigned to clear away a less-densely overgrown section of the strip, covered mainly by dead leaves and some squat bushes easily uprooted. It was clear to Isaac that the Major was still simmering with anger about his interrupted haircut.

Isaac and Pietka began working, digging out overgrown bushes, chopping at the tangled roots and digging it all out with their pickaxes. All the while, Isaac kept thinking, "I am preparing a clearing so a plane can land tomorrow and take away my Ducia. I might as well be digging my own grave."

By dusk, the group had cleared a field long enough and wide

enough for a small Russian transport plane.

The Major indicated the job was finished with a shout and a wave of his hand; then he walked down the middle of the strip, as if he was measuring the length; then he walked the width. Satisfied, he turned to the men and dismissed them.

It was almost dusk and Isaac knew he had to hurry to meet Ducia. With his pickax and shovel on his shoulder, he told Pietka he'd see him later. He turned to leave when Wasic came up to him, blocking his way. "You're always in a hurry, Sergei. If that's your real name." Isaac said nothing, but when he tried to walk around him, Wasic blocked him with the handle of the bent rake he was carrying. "Not so fast, flea."

Isaac answered curtly, "Love to talk, Wasic, but some other time."

"Trouble is you never talk about what matters."

"What's there to talk about?"

"You! Let's talk about you."

Pietka stepped in. "Sergei, get going. Let me have the tools. I'll carry them back." Isaac turned quickly, almost slapping Wasic in the face with the shovel slung over his shoulder.

"It's all right, Pietka, I can handle it," Isaac answered.

Wasic turned to Pietka. "What do you think, Pietka? I heard rumors that your good friend is no Russian. He made all that up and you played along."

Isaac threw down the tools he was carrying and confronted Wasic. "If you have anything to say about me, say it to my face. Leave Pietka out of it!"

Wasic glared straight at Isaac. "You're no Russian! I can smell your kind a mile off. I should have known from that first day I saw you. You're not one of us!"

Isaac stayed calm and answered with an amused smile, "You must be sneaking some of Kolpak's Gorilka. Be careful. That vodka is potent stuff. We'll talk when you're sober."

Wasic erupted, screaming, "You filthy Jew bastard!" He swung the rake at Isaac's face, but Isaac blocked it with his arm, grabbed the handle and pulled it out of Wasic's grip. Pietka charged into the middle, just as Wasic, in a blind fury, grabbed a knife from his belt and lunged at Isaac. But it was Pietka jumping in the middle between them who caught the knife in his side. Pietka screamed in pain, grabbing his side, blood leaking out between his fingers.

Wasic was stunned, dropped his knife and ran just as Pietka fell to the ground suddenly, dizzy and weak. Isaac screamed for help, took the cloth from his pocket that he had wrapped around his neck during the digging under the warm sun, and placed it firmly against the wound to stanch the bleeding.

The Major and Jasha came running up, having seen Wasic lunge at Isaac with a knife, thinking it was Isaac who had been hurt. But when they came up, they saw it was Pietka lying wounded on the ground. They helped lift him into Isaac's arms carefully with Isaac still pressing the cloth against the wound as they followed Isaac holding Pietka in his arms just as he had held the young Jewish boy only days ago.

Holding Pietka carefully, he walked slowly through the woods to the Partisan camp and Ducia's dugout. All the while, he kept talking to Pietka to keep him alert. "We're almost there. You got all the women waiting to fix you up, you lucky bastard. You're going to be in good hands. I promise you."

Pietka twisted in pain, but stayed conscious, saying over and over again, " I told you, Sergei. I told you."

Jasha was puzzled. "What did Pietka tell you?"

Isaac try to make light of it. "It was nothing. Just stay out of trouble."

"He should have listened to his own advice and stayed out of Wasic's way."

The Major ran ahead, hoping to catch Wasic. He kept muttering out loud, "That Wasic. He's done! He's finished. When I am through with him . . . ."

With dusk settling over Kolpak's camp, Isaac, straining with Pietka in his arms, entered Ducia's dugout and placed Pietka on the table. When he looked down at his cloth at Pietka's side, he saw it had been saturated with blood and his hand holding it was drenched up to his wrist. Soya was waiting at the table, having been alerted by the Major. But Ducia was missing.

Still, all Isaac cared about now was Pietka. His young friend was fading in and out of consciousness by now, but Isaac's pressure on the wound did slow the bleeding, and now Soya took over, cleaning the wound and applying more pressure with fresh cloths. Isaac was desperate. "If he needs blood, you can take it from me."

Soya shook her head, "We're not equipped. You know we have limits here. I'll try and keep the pressure on the wound."

At that moment, Kolpak appeared at the entrance with the Major at his side. Kolpak approached the table, his face ashen. He took Pietka's hand, squeezed it, then looked over at Soya, who smiled back reassuringly. Then, he turned to Isaac. "What got into Wasic?"

"I don't know." Isaac replied carefully. "He just went berserk."

"Was he drunk"

"I thought so, but I don't know for sure."

Then Kolpak reluctantly admitted Wasic had gotten away and is probably on his way back to his village. "I promise you, Sergei and you, Pietka, if I ever run into him, I will take care of him for good. We are supposed to fight wars, not start them!"

He looked at Soya, "Whatever must be done for Pietka, do it!" Soya nodded, then Kolpak and the Major left.

Isaac started applying cold cloths to Pietka's forehead; then taking his canteen, he wet Pietka's lips. Pietka nodded to Isaac for more. Isaac held the canteen to his lips while Pietka gulped

131

down the water, holding it with one hand to keep it steady. Then he pushed it away. He had enough for the moment. Isaac whispered to him, "Whenever you want more…whenever . . . . "

Soya stopped him. "Sergei, you've done all you can. Jasha will help. Give him the canteen. I want you to . . . to take care of yourself. Come back later."

Isaac was adamant, "No. I'll stay. Pietka and I are like brothers. I won't leave him. I'll help anyway I can."

Soya hesitated, knowing how close Isaac was to Pietka. "I understand. But if you really want to help Pietka, then the best thing is to find Ducia. I know she planned on resting down by the river. She's the best nurse in camp. Bring her to back to take care of Pietka and we'll all be grateful."

Isaac looked over a Jasha. "Jasha, you'll stay to help Soya?"

Jasha curtly replied, "He's like my brother, too. We all love Pietka."

Isaac understood. He took Pietka's hand, then kissed him on the forehead. "I'll get Ducia for you." Pietka smiled. He squirmed a bit on the table.

"Go!" Pietka raised his voice a bit, then grimaced in pain from the effort. Then quietly he repeated. "Go. Get Ducia."

Isaac took his hand, "You keep fighting, brother." Then Isaac walked off to find Ducia.

He slipped quickly down the slope leading to the eddies. With the moon a bare arc of itself, the evening had suddenly grown dark. He could hear the sound of the swirling waters before he could see the river. When he got to the bank of white pebbles, Ducia wasn't waiting for him. He looked around. There was a grove of trees above the bank to the right and a thick cluster of reeds and tall grass along the bank just to the left of him. He whispered, "Ducia? It's me." There was no response. He tried calling louder, "It's me, Sergei."

Silence at first then a trembling voice replied "Isaac?" Isaac smiled to himself, looked around in the dark to make sure no one else had followed him, then called out, "Ducia, it is me, Isaac."

He ran in the direction of the voice and found her. She was sitting near the river hidden by the tall river grass and reeds. He rushed to her, kneeled next to her and wrapped his arms around her. She leaned her head back on his shoulder. "I didn't think you were coming."

Isaac took her hand and lifted it to his lips to kiss it. But Ducia saw Isaac's hand was stained and crusted with blood. "You're hurt. That's why you're late. I knew it was something."

"It was Pietka. He's the one hurt." Isaac got up, went to the bank of the river to wash the blood stains off. "It wasn't me. It was Pietka."

Ducia stood up with some effort. "Is he . . . ?"

"He'll pull through. But . . . " He turned to Ducia, wiping his hand on his pants. "I'll take you back to him." Isaac reached out to her. She took a step and stumbled. Isaac took her hands to steady her. "I didn't want this night to end. Not like this." Isaac drew her close to him. " Our last night. . . . "

Ducia held on to Isaac tightly, desperately, afraid to slip through his embrace. Isaac had never felt her so helpless in his arms. Still, holding her as tightly and as close as this, Isaac felt that surge of sexual intimacy. But she did not respond. She held on to him more out of desperation than passion. "Isaac, I have to tell you something."

Isaac stepped back, holding both her hands firmly to steady her. "I'm listening."

"I couldn't tell you at first. I wasn't sure. "

"I know. Kolpak told me you were sick, a special case."

"He thinks he knows everything that goes on. But not this."

"He knows that you are sick, that's all." He tried to start walking with her, but she gripped his hand and wouldn't move.

"What...What is it?" He asked.

It's not that simple."

"If you're that sick, you should have told me long ago. When I saw you last with the young boy, I knew you were not well. But you said nothing."

Ducia opened up. All that was pent up inside of her poured out in an outburst of words. "I've pushed myself. For over a month. I didn't want anyone to think I couldn't do my job." Isaac was puzzled. "But it got worse. Some days I felt such pain I could barely stand or keep food down. And there were days I was sick to my stomach from morning to night. Twice I fainted in Soya's arms, the pain and bleeding was so bad. I got worried that I might be contagious, that I might be spreading it to the rest of you."

"Poor love. Why didn't you tell me?

"There was nothing to tell at first. I was scared myself and didn't want to frighten you or worry you."

"Worry me? You're all I care about. You should have told me."

"When I realized finally what it was, I thought it best to keep it quiet until . . . . "

"Quiet? You were sick. I should have been there to help. Now . . . now it's too late. By tomorrow, you'll be far away.

"I hoped, at first, I might get stronger in a month or two and then maybe . . . maybe we could leave together, leave the war behind us, maybe find America together. And when the baby came . . . . "

"The baby...?"

"Our baby. I am pregnant with our baby. I told Soya I was going to tell you once I was sure, but I've waited too long. I'm so sorry."

Isaac was silent. Then he suddenly rushed her, taking her face in his hands, kissing her over and over; then, aware that he might be hurting her and the baby, he took a step back.

She smiled, "Don't worry. I won't break. Just be easy." With that, he embraced her once again, holding her close, but carefully, tenderly.

"You can't leave now. Not with our baby."

"It's the only way. I haven't gotten stronger. The complications have gotten stronger, not me."

"You could be wrong."

"I'm not. The pain's worse and more frequent. And the blood. So much blood. Some days, when Soya covered for me, I had to lie very still. For the baby's sake. For mine, as well. It's not what I expected. It's not a good sign. And it's getting worse. I lied to Kolpak. I told him I think I am seriously ill and need an operation."

"Why?"

"Only Soya knows. And now, you. When . . . when I am back in Russia, I will tell the doctors everything. But now it has to be a secret. For my sake and for yours."

"My sake? What do I care. It's our baby! I'll shout it out all over."

"There are some here who will not take the news lightly and they will use it as an excuse to attack you, to hurt you. Jealousy, maybe, or just plain hatred for . . . whatever."

"If you mean Wasic, he's gone. For good."

"Others, like him. Not just him. Many others. It must be a secret, until . . . until . . . we're together . . . . "

"I won't let you do this."

"Dear, dear Isaac. Don't you see? I don't want to lose our baby."

"I won't let it happen."

"I love you. But I think I know what's happening. There's not much time if you want us both to survive."

"Both?"

"The baby . . . and me."

"You?"

"In Kiev, I attended women in my condition, suffering just like me. Some made it through, some . . . some didn't."

"Don't even think . . . ."

"I won't. I promise."

Isaac felt a chill. There had been too many deaths in his short life. Ducia saw the anguish in Isaac's face. She kissed him, took his hand.

"I feel stronger when I am with you. We'll go to Pietka. Maybe I can help one last time before . . . before . . . ."

The thrash and swirl of the eddies grew louder in Isaac's head, drowning out his words, thoughts, desires.

Somehow, Isaac knew it would be the last time he would hear the waters roaring, the last time he would come down to the edge of the river and find her waiting. After this night, the rushing waters of the eddies would be just a silent memory that he would take with him.

Ducia and Soya worked through the night on Pietka. It had been a superficial wound and Ducia deftly cleaned and bandaged it, so that by early morning, Pietka could sit up and felt ready to take a few steps. But when he stood up, his legs buckled. He needed some kind of support just to stand at first, so Isaac, using his pickax, cut off a bough from a white birch, trimmed it and brought it back to Pietka to use as a cane. Pietka tried to stand again, leaning on Isaac's slightly crooked white birch cane. He took a few painful steps, guided by the cane, came to the seat where the Major sat for his haircut and settled down to rest. Ducia, haggard and shaky, smiled. Soya applauded Pietka. Now they could rest.

The plane that would fly Ducia to Russia would arrive by the afternoon, so they had a few hours to recover. Ducia fell into a restless sleep in the only army cot in the dugout and Soya closed her eyes in a chair next to Pietka. Isaac went outside, sat down on the grass, leaning against the posts holding up a tarp at the entrance to the dugout, and closed his eyes, not expecting to fall asleep. He was prepared instead to stay alert through the early morning. But he couldn't fight the utter exhaustion that overtook him and he fell fast asleep.

When Kolpak woke him in the morning, shaking him roughly, Isaac jumped to his feet, grabbed his rifle and was about to point it at Kolpak, thinking he was under attack. Kolpak laughed at his confusion. Then he walked inside with Mikhail and Jasha by his side.

Isaac watched as they congratulated the women for bringing Pietka around and out of danger. Pietka himself stood up with the help of the cane and took a few steps, then told Kolpak, "I'm hungry as a bear!" Kolpak laughed. Ducia, for the moment, was free of pain, so she quickly checked over Pietka for the last time

Isaac watched all this from the entrance, but for the moment he couldn't shake off the the hazy images of what he had been dreaming just before Kolpak shook him awake. In his dream, he was back at the eddies, lost somehow in the high reeds near the river's edge, unable to move. He tried to walk, but his legs wouldn't budge. He was sinking into soft wet earth up to his ankles, then up to his knees. In a panic, he grabbed at the reeds to keep from sinking altogether but they slipped through his hands. A hand suddenly reached for him through the reeds, grabbed his right hand and tried to pull him to safety. Whose hand was it? He couldn't see and it was then that Kolpak awakened him. It was just some foolish dream, he thought, but he did feel an odd ache in his right hand, a cramp, as if he had been gripping something too tightly.

He ignored the ache and entered the dugout, patted Pietka on the shoulder for his quick recovery.

Then, the preparation began for Ducia's departure.

With the hour approaching for the plane's arrival, Isaac followed Kolpak and Mikhail down to the edge of the clearing with Ducia and Soya. Soya stayed close to Ducia, occasionally stroking her back reassuringly with one hand and carrying Ducia's small cloth satchel in her other. Soya had whispered to Isaac in the dugout that Ducia had another attack when she was alone with Soya gathering what little she would bring with her. Soya tried to comfort her, but Ducia insisted it was nothing but hunger pains. Now, on the path to the clearing, she seemed strong again as far as Isaac could tell.

At the edge of the clearing, Kolpak and Mikhail kept checking their watches and then the sky for the approaching plane. Mikhail had gotten a confirmation earlier of the plane's time of arrival. But it was late. Soya, seeing their concern, put down Ducia's satchel and walked out to Kolpak to check on the time. With Ducia standing alone, Isaac took her hand, gripping it tightly. Ducia turned and kissed him gently on the cheek. "I'll be fine. No, we'll all be fine. Talk to Soya after I leave. Kolpak will keep her informed about my . . . my location, the hospital, and everything."

Isaac kept hold of her hand tightly, not wanting to let go. Ducia leaned her body against his arm, drawing strength and passion from the feel of Isaac's body close to her. The sound of the approaching plane and Mikhail's cheers announcing its arrival ended the brief intimacy between them.

Soon everyone was crowded around Ducia, saying their farewells. Kolpak embraced her roughly, thanked her for all she had done and wished her well. Mikhail nodded his well wishes, and Soya, with tears in her eyes, embraced her and kissed her, whispering, "We will celebrate together, soon. For sure." Ducia smiled sadly in agreement. Then she turned to Isaac, gave him a gentle hug and picked up her satchel to get ready. Isaac wanted to say so much, but he choked back his words.

The small twin-engine monoplane suddenly appeared, the roar of the two propellers descended, drowning out all words and thoughts. Isaac wanted to scream against the deafening noise of the plane but he stayed silent for Ducia's sake and said nothing after the plane landed and just watched while Ducia, with the help of Soya and Kolpak, boarded the plane.

When the plane revved up its engines again, Isaac could not stand to watch anymore. He turned away while the plane took off, rumbling and roaring as it mounted into the air. He felt helpless, powerless, and alone. Another loved one had been taken from him. Maybe, he thought, this time it would not be forever.

CHAPTER TEN
DEPARTURES

For the next three weeks, with the winter approaching, many of Isaac's comrades were planning their departures for home. Though the war still raged on in the west, the rapidly expanding Russian occupation in Eastern Europe assured these partisans they would soon return to their peacetime occupations. Kolpak himself encouraged their departure. The Russian authorities had already informed him that as soon as his group was disbanded, he would be offered an official role as a commander of one of the new Russian-held territories in the East.

During these days, Isaac would approach Soya each evening to ask if she had any information from Kolpak about Ducia's health and whereabouts. But she had nothing to report. Just as the political geography of Eastern Europe was shifting daily, with new borders and new names, so was Isaac's emotional geography changing. The longer he went without hearing a word about Ducia, the greater his sense of estrangement. With his concern and anxiety building, he found he was growing more distant from those around him.

It came to a head in the fourth week of Isaac's separation from Ducia, when Pietka, fully recovered, returned with a small number of fellow partisans from a two-day sortie near the local villages to help clean out pockets of Nazi resistance. It proved uneventful.

When Pietka walked into the partisan camp, dressed for the coming cold with his padded vest and wearing his *ushanka*, a fur-lined cap with ear flaps, he had already made up his mind that it was coming time for him to return to his own village. He sought out Isaac to tell him, but he couldn't find him anywhere. Then he saw Soya coming out of Kolpak's headquarters. When Pietka approached her, he could see she had been crying.

"My God, Soya, what's wrong?"

Instead of saying a word, she put her arms around Pietka, sobbing on his shoulder.

"Tell me. Was it Kolpak? Was it something he said?"

Soya took a deep breath, stepped back from Pietka. "Where is Sergei?"

"Sergei? I just came back. I've been looking for him myself."

"We have to find him." Pietka heard desperate anguish in her voice, but was reluctant to ask her why. That tone of deep sadness in her tone pushed him back.

They searched for Isaac all through the camp, but no one had seen him. Soya even took Pietka with her down to the eddies, knowing how important it had been to Isaac and Ducia. They shouted for him up and down the bank, searched the reeds and nearby thickets, but he did not respond. Pietka could see how frantic Soya was becoming, muttering to herself, "He's somewhere. I just know he is. He has to be. He must be."

Then Soya remembered one more location. She ran ahead with Pietka barely keeping up, through the forest of birch trees and on to the clearing.

There they found Isaac, sitting there on the edge of what had been the landing strip less than a month ago. Soya turned to Pietka and motioned for him to just stay quiet for a moment. They both stood there while Isaac sat, staring at the shadows of the birch trees cast by the glow of the moon.

Not more than an hour ago, Isaac had walked into Kolpak's headquarters. Kolpak was sitting alone at his desk, sorting maps and communiqués, crumpling some and tossing them into the basket. "Sir?" Isaac's voice was tense.

Kolpak looked up. "Yes, Sergei."

"It's been over a month. I have to know what is happening with Ducia!" He spoke loudly, belligerently.

Kolpak stood up. He looked uneasy and cleared his throat, while trying to compose his thoughts. "I appreciate your interest."

"My interest? Ducia is everything to me. I don't think you can imagine how much she means to me."

"Yes. I do understand. Soya told me all about you and Ducia, in confidence."

"I'm grateful to Soya. Ducia trusts her like a sister, but I've grown weary asking her everyday. She tells me you haven't heard a word. Every day for weeks, nothing."

"Then I will talk to you directly. You deserve to know."

"So you have heard something...!"

"Sergei, why don't you sit down. Maybe I can muster up a drink for you."

"I don't need a drink or a seat. What have you heard?"

"Soya is right. Up to now, there had been nothing to report with any confidence. We've been having real problems with our radio transmissions. I was going to tell her today."

"Please, tell me. Is Ducia all right?... And the baby... what about the baby?"

"Yes, the baby. Soya never shared that detail with me. I only heard about it recently from the hospital administrator..."

"Tell me, are they both...?"

"Let let me tell you everything I was told. It will make it easier for you and for me."

"Everything?"

Kolpak began slowly, starting with Ducia's arrival at the hospital. He described how she was admitted at once and attended to immediately by the best doctors and nurses in the facility. Kolpak didn't remember what they called her condition, but it was made clear to him that the dangerous nature of her pregnancy threatened Ducia's life and the baby's. At that point, Isaac lost patience. He interrupted Kolpak's careful chronology. All he wanted to hear from Kolpak's lips was that Ducia and the baby were alive and thriving.

Kolpak realized he could not delay the truth any longer. The next words Kolpak uttered seemed unreal to Isaac, something he might have dreamt, but there was no awakening from it. Kolpak's voice echoed in his head, "Ducia died. Internal hemorrhage."

He left Kolpak abruptly, stumbling out in a daze. A few words and his life was changed. Moments before he met with Kolpak, he was filled with expectations. Weeks before he spent hours planning his future with Ducia and the child.

Before Kolpak spoke those words with such finality, Isaac still believed he would have a family waiting for him after the war. Now, he was truly alone.

He walked about the camp in no particular direction, then he found himself at the edge of the clearing. He sat on the cold ground, unable to grieve or cry. It was here, on this spot, that Ducia kissed him and left. He looked out at the open space. The moon spread an unnatural luster over the clearing. Nothing seemed real.

When he heard the distant sound of a plane, his spirits leaped. Maybe Kolpak heard it all wrong, he thought. Maybe the message from the hospital was garbled in transmission. Maybe it was someone else who died. Maybe that plane he heard was carrying Ducia back to him. But the sound of the plane grew fainter and fainter. Then silence. Ducia was gone.

It was Soya who came up behind him first. She kneeled beside him. "Sergei, I know. I'm sorry. We are all sorry."

He looked up and saw Pietka behind her. "Pietka, you got

back in one piece? I'm relieved."

Pietka was thrown by Isaac's concern for him at this moment.

"It was nothing, Sergei. No firefight, no Germans."

Isaac stood. He embraced Soya. She tried to comfort him, "It will take time, Sergei." Isaac said nothing.

A week later, Isaac told Pietka he was leaving. "Where will you go?" Pietka questioned.

"Somewhere. Anywhere. I just have to go. Away"

Pietka sensed how lost his friend was. Whether he stood still or walked for days, Isaac would be lost, Pietka was sure. There was only one option as far as Pietka was concerned. "We'll go back together. In a few weeks, before the snows. Back to my village. You'll stay with me."

Isaac was touched, but would not budge. "Pietka, you already warned me about going back. And with me by your side, you would be putting your own life in jeopardy. No. No. I've thought it through."

Unable to change his mind, Pietka offered Isaac his winter cap. Isaac waved it off. Then Pietka remembered a compass Jasha had given him. He offered it to Isaac, but he still refused. "Keep it all, Pietka. You have a long trip ahead of you as well."

That night Isaac was sure he would dream of Ducia. But when he awoke early the next morning, he couldn't remember a single moment of what he dreamt. When he looked around, he saw that Pietka had gone already.

It was a cold morning, so Isaac put on his long dark wool coat that had belonged to Novak when he was alive. Novak had been about four inches taller and fifty pounds broader than Isaac. The coat enveloped Isaac so completely, he seemed lost in it. But it would keep him warm and serve as a blanket at night.

Then Isaac put his hand in one pocket and discovered a compass, Pietka's compass. In the other deep pocket, Pietka stuffed the *ushanka* cap. Just like Pietka, Isaac thought. When he put on his friend's fur-lined cap with the ear flaps, it fit perfectly.

He wanted to start out without too much of a fuss, but Soya saw him, hugged him, and promised to light a candle for him in memory of Ducia when she was back in her church.

Soon, many who fought side by side with Isaac came up to wish him well.

Even Kolpak stopped him. He leaned his hands on Isaac's shoulder and thanked him for being a true and loyal soldier. Then, he signaled to Mikhail to hand Isaac one of his worn rucksacks carrying a stack of current maps and food stuffs and an old American Colt pistol issued to the Soviet army under the American Lend-Lease Program.

Isaac thanked Kolpak and started out, with his own satchel over one shoulder, Kolpak's rucksack over the other, and his Mauser rifle strapped across his back. He looked from behind like an itinerant peddler bearing all his worldly goods on his shoulders.

Still, there was no Pietka. Isaac eager to set out, checked the compass and started walking away from Poland towards the West.

It was then Pietka came running up behind him, holding the crooked beech cane Isaac had made for him. "Just in case you get tired." Isaac took the cane and smiled; then Pietka threw his arms around his old friend. "Don't forget me, Isaac." Isaac was startled. Pietka hadn't spoken his real name for years. "Remember you're wearing my cap and walking with my cane. Take care of them."

Isaac grinned, "Not the way you took care of me so many times, dear, dear Pietka." Holding the cane, he still managed to wrap his arms around Pietka and kissed him on both cheeks. Then he turned and started walking away from Kolpak's Partisan Brigade.

CHAPTER ELEVEN
THE WOMEN OF SLOVAKIA

After the first few weeks, Isaac lost all sense of time. Except for the little compass of Pietka's, he had no sense of direction, either. The hills, valleys and distant mountains all looked the same to him. He would check the maps Kolpak left him and try to figure out where he was. Had he left Poland? Was he in Hungary, Czechoslovakia or Slovakia? He crossed the Carpathian lowlands, the swooping valleys and rounded hills, with the hopes of finding a home that would provide him with some food.

During the day, he would avoid well-traveled roads and stayed close to the woods for cover. At night, he would seek out a thicket in the woods and sleep for a few hours, his head often resting against a gnarled root of a tree. It was against the trunk of such a tree he was forced to leave Pietka's cane behind after it snapped in two while Isaac leaned on it while trying to climb between boulders .

But Kolpak had left him an angle-head flashlight in the rucksack, so he would use it at night when needed, setting out with the help of the compass.

In late December, after many days of light snow that barely deterred him, he was suddenly buffeted and blinded by a sudden snowstorm. Straining against the pelting snow, he managed to find a barely visible dirt road, and followed it until the snow swept over it. With his head down against the whipping snow, he looked up for a moment and saw black smoke just ahead hanging like a shroud in the air. He moved towards the smoke hoping it might be from a chimney, but as he got closer, he realized it was from the aftermath of a fire that scorched the sides of a small saltbox of a house and a nearby barn. A fire that must have been quickly quenched by the snow and ice.

The barn seemed the least damaged by the fire, so Isaac trudged through the snow towards it and pushed his way inside.

He first encountered the acrid smell of smoke and wet charred wood, and when he looked around he saw that he was not alone. There, in the far corner of the barn, were a cow and a goat, both tied to a post, both nervously twitching and straining against the rope knotted about their necks.

The scrawny-ribbed goat bleated at the first sight of Isaac, then backed away as far as the rope would allow. It hid behind some cords of wood covered with hay.

But Isaac was too exhausted to spend time looking around. His whole body ached with fatigue and cold, so he slipped off his rifle and the two sacks he was carrying, wrapped Novak's coat tightly around him, pulled Pietka's cap down over his ears, and tried to stay as warm as he could while the storm raged outside. The wind and snow rattled the loose wooden slats of the barn. But somehow, out of sheer exhaustion, Isaac managed to fall asleep on a makeshift pillow of hay.

He awoke the next morning to the sound of the goat bleating. The snow had stopped, but the wind still knocked at the sides of the barn. When the goat bleated again, it made him wonder if the cow or goat had any milk left.

Finding a pail and stool in the corner, he went to the cow and tried to soothe it, knowing it was as hungry as he was. He placed the pail between his legs, firmly gripped her teats and squeezed downward. The cow looked back at him, tried to move away, but Isaac persisted and soon he heard the ring-ing of milk hitting the bucket. When he could not squeeze out anymore, he patted the cow's side again, and tilted the bucket to his lips and drank. It tasted so rich and deep, all he needed now was manna from heaven.

He looked through both his satchel and Kolpak's rucksack and found only some hard biscuits left in both. When he looked around the barn, he managed to uncover some loose halfeaten corn cobs left by the goat and, behind a pile of farm tools and a rusty plow, he found some scattered turnips and potatoes. He quickly gathered up what he could fit in his satchel, nibbling on one of the corn cobs for breakfast.

Then he decided it was time to consolidate. He put whatever was left in Kolpak's rucksack into his lighter satchel. Then, hoisting his rifle to his shoulder, he went to the door of the barn to leave. He discovered it was blocked by a snow bank wedged against it. He couldn't push it open. He looked around and found an ax lying next to the plow. Taking the ax to the door, he split the old slats of wood of the door at the top. Then he managed to crawl through the split upper half of the door and slid belly down over the snow bank. Beyond the windswept bank, the snow was only half a foot deep.

He stood up and began slogging through the snow towards the saltbox farmhouse, blackened and charred on the outside by the fire. When he came to a shattered window next to the door, he looked inside. What he saw puzzled him. There were broken chairs flung about, an overturned table, some books and paper, torn and crumpled and tossed into the simple fireplace; and there, in one corner, he saw a yellow cradle with its side ripped off and the bedding torn out. When he went to the front door, he found the simple chain lock broken. Slipping his rifle off his shoulder into his hand, he entered, rifle at the ready, but there was no one inside.

The smell of wet, smoldering wood was even stronger in the

house than in the barn. It was a one-bedroom house, so it did not take him long to check out the rooms. He noticed the beds were stripped bare of blankets. Through the window of the bedroom, he spotted the back-house privy. Again, it appeared as if someone had attacked it with an ax with such ferocity, there were just splinters left of the front.

Isaac concluded the saltbox farmhouse had been assaulted and searched brutally and then hastily set on fire when the marauders left, probably in the early hours of some snowstorm. There were no signs of struggle, no signs of life at all.

Isaac saw among the debris of broken plates, crumpled papers and shattered shards of glass, a few fragments of a larger broadside proclaiming in bold Slovakian letters, "JOIN THE FIGHT FOR INDEPENDENCE!" It was signed, THE SLOVAK NATIONAL UPRISING. He remembered talk among Kolpak's officers about such a group in Slovakia fighting for their own liberation, not only from the Germans, but from the puppet government that served at the pleasure of the Nazi regime.

After searching one more time, he found no food, no clothing—nothing to take to sustain him on his journey.

Outside, he took in a breath of clean, cold air, free of the caustic smell of wet soot and smolder, and started on his way.

For weeks after leaving the farmhouse, he kept moving, in spite of the icy knife of the wind that cut deep into his bones. He stayed away once again from snow-covered roads well-tracked by vehicles and boots, finding the darkness of night and early morning to be the best time to travel. Though he barely slept, he did not allow himself to surrender to thoughts of exhaustion or resignation. When he came across an ice-clogged river, he would manage to fill his canteen with half-frozen water. When he did not encounter a river or lake for days, he would scoop up a handful of snow and let it melt in his mouth.

Often, he would clear away the snow and ice from the base

of a tree and find in the soil some kind of root or tree nut to feed on. Those brutal months of survival after he climbed out of his family's grave in Rovno seemed to have chastened and tempered his body and spirit to endure, no matter the deprivation, fatigue, or loneliness.

One night, deep into a forest, he heard voices. He pulled his Mauser rifle from his shoulder and moved slowly away from the voices, ready to fight if seen. He caught a flickering of firelight through the trees, then the sound of laughter; then, of all things, a baby's wail. The voices were not German. What he could make out sounded vaguely like a cross between Hungarian and Czech. He stopped circling away and moved closer, still poised with rifle and pistol to fight. Then he saw them, crowded around a small fire, warming themselves. They were all women, some with fur caps and heavy sweaters, some with thick quilted shawls. One woman, looking younger than the rest, was nursing a baby, her sweater pulled up, but a heavy, embroidered blanket wrapped around the baby and herself. Isaac lowered his rifle as he peered at the women from a short distance through the trees.

Suddenly he felt the jab of a rifle in his back. A female voice behind shouted at him in a Slovakian dialect. Isaac heard some words he understood and put down his rifle and put up his hands. When he turned around, it was clear the woman guarding the group was shocked by his appearance. She jabbed the rifle into his stomach demanding his identity. Remembering Pietka's warnings about the danger he faced as a Jew even among villagers, he instinctively hid his Jewish identity once again. He called out, "Sergei, a Russian." The woman peered at him. She was dressed in a Slovakian military jacket though she wore the same fur hat with flaps as the other women.

Soon, some of the other woman surrounded him. One picked up his rifle. One searched his satchel for further proof of his identity, finding an American Colt pistol and Russian-made compass. They were clearly puzzled by what they found.

There was a moment when the first woman with the military jacket argued fiercely with the others as she prodded Isaac forward with her rifle towards the fire. It was clear to Isaac from her words that this woman wanted him killed. She held up his Mauser rifle to make her point that Isaac was a German, a Nazi soldier.

The younger woman nursing her baby stayed seated by the fire and said nothing, just cradled her baby, humming and whispering soothingly until the baby was asleep.

Then, a sturdy, taller woman grabbed Isaac by the shoulder. She asked, holding him tightly, "Why are you here?"

Isaac looked around, kept holding his hands high as he begged in broken Russian, "Russian Partisan. Kolpak Brigade. Lost." His voice was hoarse. He realized he had not spoken a word to another human being in so long, he didn't even recognize his own voice. But he cleared his throat and repeated the clipped phrases in Polish in hopes that some words would be understood.

The woman holding him, shook her head "Yes," as if she understood. Then, for some reason, she pointed to his face and she scowled, "Animal." Isaac ran his fingers over his now long and grizzled beard and his unruly hair that had grown over his ears. He had not looked at a reflection of himself in months. He tried to smile sheepishly, made a gesture with hands, apologizing for what he realized was his wild, almost savage look.

Then the woman turned to the others and reassured them that Isaac had been a Russian partisan fighting against the Nazis but was clearly lost. The one with the military jacket growled in protest, sat down disgruntled and angry, and laid her rifle across her lap.

The rest of the women continued to stare at him with some

disbelief, but then the one with the baby shouted something about food and the others seemed to agree, except for the woman with the military garb.

The sturdy woman led him to the fire and another offered him some warm coffee in a chipped cup which he grabbed with both hands and gulped down. Another brought him a carrot and a piece of cheese which he devoured just as quickly.

While he ate, he noticed on the ground next to the nursing woman the same broadside he saw in the smoldering farmhouse, proclaiming independent Slovakia and declaring an uprising. Then he knew. These women—mothers, wives, daughters—were fighting against their own puppet government and the Germans. Maybe their men had been killed or captured. Maybe the woman with the baby once lived in that half-burnt farmhouse with the splintered cradle. It was clear to Isaac that he was back among partisans.

For a week, he traveled with the women, learning some of their names on the way. It was on the third day with them that Tereza, an older-looking woman with crooked teeth and a face deeply creased, gave him a some kind of fabric shears with a serrated edge so that he could at least cut off some his hair and trim his beard. He chopped away, his dark, knotted hair and beard falling in clumps around his feet, but when it came to the back of his head, he could only snip away blindly. Tereza smiled at his awkward effort and took the shears gently from his hand, gesturing that she would take over. She directed him to a large boulder, had him sit, and she went to work cutting his hair from behind him. He thought for a fleeting second of the many times Ducia would cut his hair pressing close to his body, gently moving the scissor and her hand lovingly about his head. But the image faded quickly when the older woman started to cough violently. Isaac turned and tried to comfort her, but she raised her hand, and gave him back the scissors to finish the job. She left, coughing breathlessly.

He found out a few days later that the women were seeking to escape from both the local Slovakian army and the Germans. Their hope was to find the Russian Army that had come to liberate Slovakia. Except for Eliska with her rifle and military jacket and the tall, sturdy woman, Jarmilla, who carried a Walther pistol, the rest were not armed.

Jarmilla had told Isaac earlier that these woman had lost their husbands, children, and homes to the war, escaping with whatever they could carry. She pointed out Eliska as an example. Eliska had watched as Slovakian soldiers charged into their house and dragged out her husband and son to be executed for treason. The husband had been a soldier himself, but had rebelled against the brutality of the government and refused to wear the uniform anymore. After they were taken away, she took her husband's military uniform with the Slovakian insignia on it and his rifle and escaped into the forest to join the uprising. From that day on, she wore his military jacket out of protest, Jarmilla claimed.

He looked upon these women with a great deal of respect and admiration. They were survivors just like him. He thought about staying with them just to help them find the Russian Army, so they could feel once again that their country would be safe for future families. It was something he felt Ducia would want him to do.

But late one night, at the end of that week with them, he overheard Eliska and Jarmilla talking. Isaac had decided early on in his stay with them that he would guard them at night, staying a short distance from where they slept. Often, he was too far away to hear them whispering. But this time the two women were taking loud enough for Isaac to hear. He heard them complain about the danger their Jewish neighbors had caused them when the Slovkian army ordered the resettlement of all Jews for their own safety. Eliska couldn't understand why so many of the Jews refused to leave their homes. "It was for their own good," he heard Jarmilla conclude. "It would have made things easier for the rest of us." They both agreed that it was after the Jews refused to cooperate that the Slovakian Army, under orders from the country's President, began a campaign of wholesale slaughter of the Jews. "If only they had cooperated and left peacefully," Jarmilla emphasized. "They wouldn't have put the rest of us in such danger once the killing began." Isaac heard other woman clucking in assent.

What he heard made it imperative for him to leave, to find a country and a people where he could become Isaac safely again.

That next morning, he announced that he had no choice but to leave them, reluctantly, of course. He lied, saying he felt it was his duty to rejoin his partisan brigade back in Poland.

They did not question his patriotism, and so he gathered up his satchel and rifle to depart. But then, Ruzena, the nursing mother, asked him to hold her baby girl while she went off into forest to relieve herself. It was the first time she had ever offered the baby girl to him. She told him in a shy, quiet voice, she wanted to tell her daughter, when the girl was old enough to understand, that a great Russian fighter had once held her in his arms. It would be a blessing. Before Isaac could say anything, Ruzena held the baby in her outstretched arms in front of his face. The women all watched breathlessly. Isaac had no choice. He slipped off his rifle, put down his satchel and took the baby in his arms. She sighed gratefully and turned towards the woods.

As soon as the mother left, the baby started crying. Isaac cradled the baby awkwardly at first, then gently rocked her and patted her back tenderly. He began quietly humming a tune his mother sang to him when he was a child. It seemed to soothe her. She closed her eyes and Isaac nestled the baby even deeper in his arms. The women watched and smiled approvingly. For a few minutes, Isaac was a father. He felt nothing else but the gentle weight of the baby in his arms, heard nothing but her soft murmuring as she slept, and thought of nothing but the peacefulness of the moment.

But with the return of the mother, Isaac returned to his solitary state. He slipped on his rifle again, lifted his satchel and started to leave when Eliska, the one who had wanted him dead a week before, came up to him, shook his hand, gave him a kiss on his cheek and offered him a few packs of her husband's military rations, which he took and put in his satchel, thanking her. Then waving to all, he started out, alone once more.

CHAPTER TWELVE
THE CURE OF ORANGES

Again Isaac traveled at night, staying close to the forest when he could. Using Kolpak's map and Pietka's compass, he hoped to skirt the borders of Hungary and Austria and travel slightly south and west towards Italy. Well into his third week, he began to hear the sounds of distant artillery and bombings. He could even feel the reverberations of the earth under his feet.

Then, weeks later, as he moved many kilometers farther south and west, the tremors ceased and the sound of explosions grew fainter.

One morning, he crawled out of his forest retreat where he hid in the shadows of towering pine trees and saw, for the first time, snowy peaks and crags of what he assumed were the Dolomites, according to the map. If he was traveling in the right direction, he was approaching the northeast boundary between Italy and Yugoslavia.

He could feel the mild touch of the morning sun and could sense the loosening grip of winter on the land. The wind blew softer, smelled sweeter and cleaner.

But it was short lived. A few days later, he heard the sound of planes and the explosions of war again that brought with it on the wind the sour smell of sulphur and charcoal. The smell always reminded Isaac of Hell's own brimstone and fire. This time it felt closer; the earth rolled and quaked beneath him. He pushed on nevertheless, kilometer after kilometer, until he heard the rattle and pop of gunshots. There was a firefight nearby.

Isaac was forced to inch along now, wary of some skirmish that might be just ahead. He made some calculations and thought he was moving away from the battles, climbing with great effort the foothills of the mountains, sometimes crawling over rocks jutting out from the grass. Then, as he came to the top of a small hill, he heard what sounded like military commands.

He dropped to the ground, staying as flat and invisible as possible, and crawled on his stomach, dragging himself with his hands and knees towards the crest of the hill. When he came to the top, he looked down into a valley covered with scrub trees and pine. A dirt road ran through it and, not too distant from Isaac, to the east, he saw a file of soldiers slogging wearily, growing nearer and nearer.

As they came closer, Isaac saw their uniforms were khaki-colored, drab brown, and they were in full gear with holstered pistols at their side, canteens hanging from a strap across their chests, and semi-automatic rifles, which they held in front of them, poised and ready.

At first, he couldn't identify their country of origin. The uniform did look familiar but he had to be certain. Then he saw a group in the middle of the file, stripped of their weapons, guarded closely by the other soldiers. Isaac knew they were prisoners, captured by these soldiers. They wore torn and half-buttoned greenish-blue jackets, the color the Germans called Feldbluse. It was suddenly clear to Isaac. They were German prisoners.

Then, one of the German prisoners tried to break free from the ranks and make a run for it. A voice rang, "You ain't going nowhere, Kraut!" As his words echoed, the same soldier caught up with the prisoner and smashed him on the head with the butt of his rifle. The German went down, his hands on his head, muttering in pain. The soldier forced him up, poking him with his rifle and leading him back into the group of fellow prisoners. With the sweep of his gun pointing at the prisoners, the soldier shouted, "Next one tries that, gets plugged for good! Kaput! Get it?"

It was the voice of an American, Isaac was sure. He knew enough English from his school days and his reading, but especially from American movies with Polish subtitles. It was in the dark of Rovno's stifling movie theatres where Isaac had heard and remembered the clipped, edgy language of those American actors with their nervous rhythms, inflections, and raw diction. He felt a surge of energy. These were American soldiers! He wanted to shout to them, "God bless you," in English, but he hadn't spoken or studied that tongue in so long, he was not sure it would come out right. He remembered speaking it to himself as a schoolboy after every American movie. But this was no movie, and he was no longer a schoolboy.

Nevertheless, Isaac jumped to his feet, unafraid, eager to join them. He had traveled so long, so far and now he felt he had arrived at the right place.

He walked carefully down the slope of the valley, hoping they would see him and welcome him. But a battle-weary American captain at the head of the line looked up, saw this ragged, odd figure coming towards his men wearing an oversize dark coat, a bulky fur cap, and carrying a nondescript satchel, with a rifle strapped to his shoulder. The captain's mind raced. This wild character could be a deserter or a sniper, disguised as a peasant, concealing beneath the ample drape of the coat or in his satchel or even under his strange fur hat, a grenade or some kind of explosive. The captain erupted, yelling at his men, "If the son of a bitch up there goes for his rifle, shoot him! Carlton and Solowitz, you know what to do!" The two soldiers dropped to their knees and took aim with Isaac clearly in their crosshairs.

Isaac was stunned. He threw up his hands and shouted out instinctively in Polish "Friend!" The captain did not understand. "Drop your rifle!"

The American soldier called Solowitz, recognizing Isaac's Slavic word, yelled at him in a garbled mix of Polish and Yiddish to drop to his knees and throw down his rifle.

Issac understood both the captain and Solowitz and dropped to his knees and threw his rifle to the ground.

The captain, still wary, shouted, "Throw down your bag, that fur cap and your filthy coat." Before Solowitz could attempt to translate, Isaac dropped his satchel, pulled off his hat and slipped off his coat, holding it open to show that there was nothing inside. "Start walking towards us slowly! Hands up!" Isaac walked carefully down the slope, his hands above his head.

The captain yelled out once more. "Solowitz, check him out. Carlton, get everything he dropped. "

What Isaac had hoped would be his deliverance had turned into a nightmare of mistaken identity. Forced to march under guard with the German prisoners, he tried not to look at their faces. He could hear the two Nazi officers among the prisoners confiding in whispers to each other in what Isaac recognized as High German. They muttered low insults directed at him. "Look. Dumb, filthy Polish sewer rat. Speaks with gutter accent. Marching next to us. Disgusting." Isaac understood every word but feigned ignorance. At one point, a German soldier deliberately pushed him. Isaac stumbled, almost losing his balance. An American soldier came up to him and shoved him with his rifle back in line. Isaac felt the bile rising in his gut against the German prisoner. He clenched his fist and jammed it against his side to hide his anger; then, turning to the German who pushed him, Isaac nodded and, speaking deliberately in the dialect of an uneducated Polish peasant, apologized for bumping into the German. The German prisoner laughed derisively at him and Isaac, sadly but knowingly, had adopted a new deceptive guise once more, to be humiliated by the arrogant and scornful haughtiness of the Nazis. In this way he hoped the Americans would see he was not an adversary, but a target of the Nazis just like them.

After an hour's march, they entered the main square of a small town. Isaac saw around him the grotesque remnants of what once were homes and buildings, now either bombed out piles of rubble or jagged, leaning slabs that once were walls of buildings.

A building at the head of the square was least damaged of all, though there were shattered windows and gouges in the walls from bullets and explosives. Above the main door, Isaac could see a partial word, "MUNI -" though the rest of the inlaid words had been lost, shaken loose by explosions.

The soldiers led them to the side of the building. At that moment, a small group of local townspeople came out of nowhere and rushed towards them, jeering and spitting at the German prisoners, threatening to attack them. The soldiers were thrown off guard when suddenly, some broke through the ranks, cursing and shouting. Two of them charged the two Nazi officers and grappled with them. The Nazi officers shouted in protest while they struggled until the American soldiers charged the locals and separated them at gunpoint from the officers. All through the melee, Isaac stood to one side, next to an American soldier, calmly watching and savoring the attack on these Nazis.

When the group dispersed, the guards led them into the building and down a small corridor where heavily armed guards stood in front of a locked wooden door. The guards opened it and Isaac and the German prisoners were ordered into the room. The room had once been used for some kind of municipal storage but was now stripped bare of any furniture or file cabinet, except some yellow legal documents scattered about the floor. There was one bulb high up in the ten-foot ceiling and one small barred window at the very top.

As Isaac entered, side by side with Nazi officers and soldiers, the Germans quickly went to one corner of the room, avoiding Isaac, glaring at him with such repulsion, he had to repress the seething urge to attack them with his fists, foolish and futile as it might be.

Instead he sat, hunched in the corner. At one point, a guard opened the door, with another behind him with his rifle held in front of him, and pointed at one of the Nazi officers and shouted his name, "Bock!" The officer did not respond. "Bock! You!" The Nazi officer turned his back to the guard and seemed to be conferring with the other officer, though Isaac thought he saw the one named Bock secretly hand some items to the other. The guard shouted at him once more. "Bock. Now!" The Nazi turned, snapped to attention and responded curtly and sharply, demanding respect, "Colonel Fedor von Bock, sir!" The Guard shrugged and said again, "Okay. Damn it! You, Colonel Fedor von Bock. For questioning, damn it!" The colonel marched out crisply with the guard. He was the heaviest and tallest of the group of prisoners. Clearly a seasoned colonel in the Nazi Wehrmacht, Isaac thought, from all his stripes and decorations. The other Nazi officer drew back, leaning against the wall, waiting for the guards to leave and the door to be closed and locked.

At that moment, this officer gathered his soldiers around him, handing one of them what Isaac could now see was a small pistol and giving another what looked like a combat knife. Then the officer, speaking in hushed tones, but loud enough for Isaac to hear, outlined the plan of attack. He did not seem to concern himself about Isaac listening. He was sure this lowly Polish peasant squatting in the opposite corner couldn't understand his literate and educated German. But Isaac understood every word.

Isaac heard and understood from what the officer said that a few members of the crowd that had assaulted the Germans outside the building were Nazi sympathizers. They pretended to grapple with the Nazi officers, but in truth, got close enough to slip them weapons to be used for their escape.

Isaac pretended to be oblivious to them, hunched down in the corner, but he listened intently. The officer alerted the other soldiers that the moment they heard the unlocking of the door, the armed men would stand against the wall by the door so that when it was opened and the Americans stepped in to return the colonel, they would attack them, subdue them and hold them as hostages. Then the officer, glancing at Isaac, made it clear that if necessary he would kill the Polish pig to show the Americans they were serious. The German soldiers nodded in approval. Isaac caught the officer glancing at him from time to time, smug and confident that Isaac would make the perfect scapegoat.

Isaac realized he could not stand by and let it happen. They assumed he would be a passive, frightened spectator. But he knew he had to act, somehow, in some way. He waited, constructing in his head the tactics he would employ to protect the Americans and foil the Nazis. He knew it was desperate, but he had no choice. There was no other option but to act.

So he waited. It seemed to him many hours, but in truth, it was less than an hour later when he heard the guards outside unlocking the door. Quickly, the Nazi officer and the two armed soldiers ran to both sides of the door. The officer and one of the soldiers pointed their pistols in readiness towards the door, while the other soldier gripped his knife, ready to pounce on the guards when they brought the colonel into the room.

A second before the door was opened, Isaac acted. He bolted from the corner slammed his shoulder against the door to keep it shut, then grabbed the gun from the startled German soldier and kicked him away. At the same time, he yelled in his heavily accented English, "The Nazis have guns!" The Nazi officer at the other side of the door opened fire on Isaac just as he twisted around to face him. The bullet struck Isaac's left arm, but he didn't flinch and started firing at the Nazi officer wildly, forcing him to retreat to a far corner.

One of the German soldiers came at Isaac with his combat knife just as the door flung wide open and three American guards with semi-automatics charged in. They saw the German lunging at Isaac with his knife and opened fire on him, killing him. At the same time, the Nazi officer started shooting at them from a far corner in desperation, but before he could get a second round off, he was hit by a spray of bullets from the semi-automatics. The other German soldiers dropped to their knees and raised their arms in surrender. Isaac still held the pistol pointed at the German soldier, who was on his knees with his arms raised. Isaac, for the first time, realized his left arm was bleeding and burning with pain, but he kept the pistol pointed at the soldier. When a guard tried to take the pistol from Isaac, he had to forcibly wrench it from Isaac's intense grip.

The Germans were herded to a corner of the room, forced to their knees with their backs to the door while guards searched them for weapons.

The Nazi officer and the soldier who had come at Isaac with a knife were both dead. Isaac, bleeding badly, fell to his knees, too weak to stand. One of the guards came up to him and spoke, "You did all right, boy. You're going to be fine. The medics are coming."

Isaac looked up at his face, smiled, and stammered to him in English, "I'm . . . I'm Isaac."

The American soldier put his arm around him for support. "Glad to know you, Isaac." Hearing his name spoken in friendship by another, he relaxed and let the shock of the wound and the years of survival sweep over him until he succumbed to it at last, losing consciousness.

What he remembered after that was a blurred, wavering cloud of images—he thought he saw Colonel Bock, handcuffed and kneeling in the corridor as he went past, then an image of a young American medic with glasses who kept smiling at him, running alongside his stretcher. There was the vague sound of doors opening and closing, and, finally, a bright, glaring light with new faces leaning over him, men in white surgical gowns with white masks over their noses and mouths. Then, Isaac fell into a deep sleep.

Somewhere in the hours or days that he slept, he started to dream again, so vividly it felt real. He would remember this one dream for the rest of his life. It began with his family sitting around the polished dining room table in his Rovno home. It had been set for a feast. There was a silver tray holding a large challah, with its buttery twists and smooth sheen, next to a great porcelain casserole steaming with his mother's stew. At the head of the table sat his beloved Grandfather sitting in the high-back chair, holding on to his ebony cane with the brass handle. Next to him, Grandmother and Aunt; and farther down the table, his older brother, the beloved doctor, and his wife. His mother and father appeared at the entrance to the dining room; she, in her flowery apron; he, holding a basket laden with oranges, announcing that he had brought them back from Brest just for this special night. Oranges! The family cheered and laughed. Isaac remembered even in his dream how his father would bring back oranges whenever anyone in the family was stricken with a bad cold or fever. Mother would slice up the fruit and make the sick member eat a whole orange including the rind once a day until they recovered. Isaac believed oranges would cure most anything that ailed his family. They were all there, except for Isaac.

Grandfather's gravel-pitched voice recited the prayer for the bread, then he cut the challah with an ivory-handled bread knife, his hands shaking a bit. Then, looking around the table, he joked, "Where is our boy, Izziela? Too proud to eat with us?" They all laughed.

For a moment, the dream sputtered; sounds of other voices clamoring to interrupt broke into Isaac's sleep. Then, the dream was back again in the dining room. There was a slamming of the door, the sound of a gust of wind, and Isaac was suddenly standing at the table, his arms around a pale and sickly Ducia, who held a small child in her arms, wrapped so tightly in a quilted blanket the baby could not be seen. But Isaac could hear the tiny, constricted cries of the infant. Everyone at the table stood up and held out their arms in welcome. Ducia had tears in her eyes. She turned to Isaac and kissed him on the cheek. Then Isaac's mother came up to them, seeing that Ducia was growing too weak to hold the infant, and gently lifted the crying baby out of Ducia's arms, saying, "Do not worry, dear. The oranges will cure everything." In his dream, he did not know if his mother meant curing Ducia, the infant or Isaac himself. It did not matter. It all felt so good and true and perfect. He pulled Ducia even closer, holding on to her tightly so she could never slip away. But the image faded. He heard a voice speaking in a mix of Polish and Yiddish, and Isaac awoke. It was the American soldier, Solowitz.

"What's wrong?" Solowitz asked. Isaac was confused. He realized he was on an army cot, his arm heavily bandaged.

"You're crying, Isaac. Does your arm hurt that much?"

Isaac realized he was crying. But it wasn't the pain of the operation, it was the dream. It was seeing his family again and seeing Ducia for the first time since her death, feeling her close and knowing she was gone. He was crying for so much for the first time, but Solowitz would never understand.

Then he realized, the American called him Isaac. He was Isaac again. Solowitz spoke again in a language stew of Polish and Yiddish, "You're a hero, Isaac. Do you know that?"

Isaac looked at him through bleary eyes. In his distant memory of English, he replied, "Talk to me in English, please."

Solowitz laughed and replied in English. "You're still a hero!"

Isaac replied, "Your name, what is it?"

The soldier smiled. "Solowitz. Nathan Solowitz. You can call me Nat."

Isaac took Nat's hand and shook it. Even though his English was often interspersed with Polish and Yiddish dialect, he knew Nat would be able to follow, "I'm Isaac Gochman. A Jew from Rovno, Poland.

"Welcome Isaac Gochman, a Jew from Rovno, Poland. I'm Nat Solowitz, a Jew from Pelham Parkway, The Bronx, New York.

Isaac sighed. "It has been so long since I said my full name out loud."

Nathan Solowitz seem to understand. "The captain has ordered me to take good care of you while I am still stationed here. First, you have to get healed real good. The doctor said you were so malnourished, you should have died months ago. We got to build you up."

"I'll try," Isaac promised.

Nat laughed. "I went to a lot of trouble, but I managed to get you one orange. You kept muttering about oranges all those days you were feverish and delirious. But I figured it couldn't hurt. Trouble is, most of the groves have been destroyed. I think this was the captain's last orange. Enjoy it, Isaac." Solowitz stood, saluted and left.

Isaac looked at the side table and saw orange slices in a tin bowl. The memory of that vivid dream was still fresh in his mind. He reached for a slice, put it in his mouth to savor. And the taste and the memory of it all came rushing back and he began to cry one last time for Ducia, for his unborn child and for his family.

A week later, Isaac was out of bed and moving around. Solowitz came by at least once a day to check on him and remarked how his English was improving by leaps and bounds. Isaac was puzzled by the phrase "leaps and bounds," but knew there were a million new American idioms he would be hearing from now on.

It was on the last day before Nathan and his squadron moved north that Isaac was told he would be going to The Bronx, New York. Nathan had made arrangements with cousins there to sponsor Isaac. With the help of the captain and his immediate superior, a two-star general, he was granted an emergency visa and would leave in a week on a transport plane to England and from there on a troop ship to America.

Nathan came to him one last time. He was loaded down with all his gear, about to move out. Isaac still had his left arm in a sling. Nathan gave him a sheet of paper with his cousins' names and addresses. They both embraced. Then Nathan said good-bye with a final remark, "Don't forget, Isaac from Rovno, save me some oranges."

And Isaac didn't forget. A year later, when Nathan Solowitz disembarked from the troop ship, *Ernie Pyle,* Isaac was there on the pier, greeting him with a basket of oranges.

AUTHOR'S NOTE

I met the real Isaac in the late 1980's after my agent insisted I listen to his compelling story. Isaac was nearing 70 when I met him but from the first encounter to the last, he was a genuinely vital individual, at peace with himself and with the world around him.

For many months, I sat with him in his modest Bronx kitchen as he related the story of his incredible survival, sharing photos, war memorabilia and hand-written notes from his past with me.

Often when I came in the late afternoon to his apartment, he would first offer me a glass of Schnapps, then talk leisurely and proudly of some of his accomplishments after the war. Given his impressive fluency with many languages—he could read and speak English, Polish, Russian, Hebrew, Yiddish, German, Ukrainian the U.S. Information Agency invited him to be an international host at the 1958 Brussels Worlds Fair .

During one meeting he illustrated his prowess as the most effective demolition expert among the Russian partisans by showing me how he would prepare the dynamite explosives used to destroy Nazi troop and freight trains. He demonstrated, with cardboard rolls as his dynamite, tying them together with string and showing me how short the fuse was and where the explosive would be placed on the tracks. I kept thinking how surreal it seemed: Here I was with this gentle, calm figure showing me so matter-of-factly the finer points of blowing up Nazi trains while we sat in his small, modest kitchen a few stories above the traffic noise of the Cross Bronx Expressway.

When he talked of the Nazi genocide, the loss of home, country and all of his beloved family in one horrific night, he would soften his tone to a whisper and a strain of anguish would seep into his voice while he went on to describe the massacre and the unimaginable hardships he faced in the Polish Forest.

Then, when he talked of Ducia, the partisan nurse, there was both ardor and deep sadness in his voice. He spoke of how his relationship with her grew from youthful infatuation to love and intimacy, transcending religious differences.

It was during those meetings he gave me the rare photo of the Russian partisan group with Ducia seated in front at the center between his best friend, Pietka, and him, the young Isaac, looking at her wistfully.

Through it all, in spite of the suffering he endured, he was always at peace with himself, having earned a wisdom beyond my limited compass of life.

Though I never forgot Isaac or his story, it has taken me almost three decades to shape, reshape and finish the novel. My goal as the writer has always been to invest character and moment with believable reality. For that reason, I have taken narrative and artistic liberties throughout.

Still, it has always been the memory of Isaac's indomitable spirit that guided and inspired me over these years to finally create a world that could not have existed without him.

Isaac Gochman after the war, in America.

Front and center are Isaac, Ducia and Pietka, Kolpak's Brigade, 1944.

CPSIA information can be obtained
at www.ICGtesting.com
Printed in the USA
LVOW12*1951291217
561261LV00001B/15/P